TOM SWIFT AND HIS WAR TANK;
OR,
DOING HIS BIT
FOR UNCLE SAM

By
VICTOR APPLETON

Tom Swift And His War Tank;
Or,
Doing His Bit For Uncle Sam

by **Victor Appleton**

ISBN: 978-93-57482-97-4

Published by

DOUBLE 9 BOOKS

2/13-B, Ansari Road
Daryaganj, New Delhi – 110002
info@double9books.com
www.double9books.com
Tel. 011-40042856

This book is under public domain

ABOUT THE AUTHOR

"The Stratemeyer Syndicate is fascinating because of how many well-known series they created under several pen identities, such Victor Appleton.

The most well-known series published under the Victor Appleton identity is Tom Swift, and like the other series ""authored"" by Victor Appleton, the plots for this one were created from outlines by ghostwriters. A second series was created because Tom Swift was so well-liked. The Syndicate determined in 1954 that the first series' Tom Swift had a teenage son who emulated his father's inventiveness. Compared to the first series, this second one has more space-related themes (which featured airships and other inventions appropriate to its time period). Victor Appleton II, the author's son who was created in the same way as Tom Swift was, was not a real-life person like the original pen name Victor Appleton."

CONTENTS

Chapter I
Past Memories

Ceasing his restless walk up and down the room, Tom Swift strode to the window and gazed across the field toward the many buildings, where machines were turning out the products evolved from the brains of his father and himself. There was a worried look on the face of the young inventor, and he seemed preoccupied, as though thinking of something far removed from whatever it was his eyes gazed upon.

"Well, I'll do it!" suddenly exclaimed Tom. "I don't want to, but I will. It's in the line of 'doing my bit,' I suppose; but I'd rather it was something else. I wonder—"

"Ha! Up to your old tricks, I see, Tom!" exclaimed a voice, in which energy and friendliness mingled pleasingly. "Up to your old tricks!"

"Oh, hello, Mr. Damon!" cried Tom, turning to shake hands with an elderly gentleman—that is, elderly in appearance but not in action, for he crossed the room with the springing step of a lad, and there was the enthusiasm of youth on his face. "What do you mean—my old tricks?"

"Talking to yourself, Tom. And when you do that it means there is something in the wind. I hope, as a sort of side remark, it isn't rain that's in the wind, for the soldiers over at camp have had enough water to set up a rival establishment with Mr. Noah. But there's something going on, isn't there? Bless my memorandum book, but don't tell me there isn't, or I shall begin to believe I have lost all my deductive powers of reasoning! I come in here, after knocking two or three times, to which you pay not the least attention, and find you mysteriously murmuring to yourself.

"The last time that happened, Tom, was just before you started to dig the big tunnel—No, I'm wrong. It was just before you started for the Land of Wonders, as we decided it ought to be called. You were talking to yourself then, when I walked in on you, and—Say, Tom!" suddenly exclaimed Mr. Damon eagerly, "don't tell me you're going off on another wild journey like that—don't!"

"Why?" asked Tom, smiling at the energy of his caller.

"Because if you are, I'll want to go with you, of course, and if I go it means I'll have to start in as soon as I can to bring my wife around to my way of thinking. The last time I went it took me two weeks to get her to consent, and then she didn't like it. So if—"

"No, Mr. Damon," interrupted Tom, "I don't count on going on any sort of a trip—that is, any long one. I was just getting ready to take a little spin in the Hawk, and if you'd like to come along—"

"You mean that saucy little airship of yours, Tom, that's always trying to sit down on her tail, or tickle herself with one wing?"

"That's the Hawk!" laughed Tom; "though that tickling business you speak of is when I spiral. Don't you like it?"

"Can't say I do," observed Mr. Damon dryly.

"Well, I'll promise not to try any stunts if you come along," Tom went on.

"Where are you going?" asked his friend.

"Oh, no place in particular. As you surmised, I've been doing a bit of thinking, and—"

"Serious thinking, too, Tom!" interrupted Mr. Damon. "Excuse me, but I couldn't help overhearing what you said. It was something about going to do something though you didn't want to, and that it was part of your 'bit'. That sounds like soldier talk. Are you going to enlist, Tom?"

"No."

"Um! Well, then—"

"It's something I can't talk about, Mr. Damon, even to you, as yet," Tom said, and there was a new quality in his voice, at which his friend looked up in some surprise.

"Oh, of course, Tom, if it's a secret—"

"Well, it hasn't even got that far, as yet. It's all up in the air, so to speak. I'll tell you in due season. But, speaking of the air, let's go for a spin. It may drive some of the cobwebs out of my brain. Did I hear you say you thought it would rain?"

"No, it's as clear as a bell. I said I hoped it wouldn't rain for the sake of the soldiers in camp. They've had their share of wet weather, and, goodness knows, they'll get more when they get to Flanders. It seems to do nothing but rain in France."

"It is damp," agreed Tom. "And, come to think of it, they are going to have some airship contests over at camp to-day—for the men who are being trained to be aviators, you know. It just occurred to me that we might fly over there and watch them."

"Fine!" cried Mr. Damon. "That's the very thing I should like. I'll take a chance in your Hawk, Tom, if you'll promise not to try any spiral stunts."

"I promise, Mr. Damon. Come on! I'll have Koku run the machine out and get her ready for a flight to Camp. It's a good day for a jaunt in the air."

"Get out the Hawk, Koku," ordered the young inventor, as he motioned to a big man—a veritable giant—who nodded to show he understood. Koku was really a giant, one of a race of strange beings, and Tom Swift had brought the big man with him when he escaped from captivity, as those will remember who have read that book.

"Going far, Tom?" asked an aged man, coming to the door of one of the many buildings of which the shed where the airship was kept formed one.

"Not very far, Father," answered the young inventor. "Mr. Damon and I are going for a little spin over to Camp Grant, to see some aircraft contests among the army birdmen."

"Oh, all right, Tom. I just wanted to tell you that I think I've gotten over that difficulty you found with the big carburetor you were working on. You didn't say what you wanted it for, except that it was for a heavy duty gasolene engine, and you couldn't get the needle valve to work as you'd like. I think I've found a way."

"Good, Dad! I'll look at it when I come back. That carburetor did bother me, and if I can get that to work—well, maybe we'll have something soon that will—"

But Tom did not finish his sentence, for Koku was getting the aircraft in operation and Mr. Damon was already taking his place behind the pilot's seat, which would be occupied by Tom.

"All ready, are you, Koku?" asked the young inventor.

"All ready, Master," answered the giant.

There was a roar like that of a machine gun as the Hawk's engine spun the propeller, and then, after a little run across the sod, it mounted into the air, carrying Tom and Mr. Damon with it.

"Mind you, Tom, no stunts!" called the visitor to the young inventor through the speaking tube apparatus, which enabled a conversation to be carried on, even above the roar of the powerful engine. "Bless my overshoes! if you try, looping the loop with me—"

"I won't do anything like that!" promised Tom.

Away they soared, swift as a veritable hawk, and soon, after there had unrolled below their eyes a succession of fields and forest, there came into view rows and rows of small brown objects, among which beings, like ants, seemed crawling about.

"There's the Camp!" exclaimed Tom.

"I see," and Mr. Damon nodded.

As they approached, they saw, starting up from a green space amid the brown tents, what appeared to be big bugs of a dirty white color splotched with green.

"The aircraft—and they have camouflage paint on," said Tom. "We can watch 'em from up here!"

Mr. Damon nodded, though Tom could not see him, sitting in front of his friend as he was.

Up and up circled the army aircraft, and they seemed to bow and nod a greeting to the Hawk, which was soon in the midst of them. Tom and Mr. Damon, flying high, though at no great speed, looked at the maneuvers of the veterans and the learners—many of whom might soon be engaging the Boches in far-off France.

"Some of 'em are pretty good!" called Tom, through the tube. "That one fellow did the loop as prettily as I've ever seen it done," and Tom Swift had a right to speak as one of authority.

Tom and his friend watched the aircraft for some time, and then started off in a long flight, attaining a high speed, which, at first, made Mr. Damon gasp, until he became used to it. He was no novice at flying, and had even operated aeroplanes himself, though at no great height.

Suddenly the Hawk seemed to falter, almost as does a bird stricken by a hunter's gun. The craft seemed to hang in the air, losing motion as though about to plunge to earth unguided.

"What's the matter?" cried Mr. Damon.

"One of the control wires broken!" was Tom's laconic answer. "I'll have to volplane down. Sit tight, there's no danger!"

Mr. Damon knew that with so competent a pilot as Tom Swift in the forward seat this was true, but, nevertheless, he was a bit nervous until he felt the smooth, gliding motion, with now and then an upward tilt, which showed that Tom was coming down from the upper regions in a series of long glides. The engine had stopped, and the cessation of the thundering noise made it possible for Tom and his passenger to talk without the use of the speaking tube.

"All right?" asked Mr. Damon.

"All right," Tom answered, and a little later the machine was rolling gently over the turf of a large field, a mile or so from the camp.

Before Tom and Mr. Damon could get out of their seats, a man, seemingly springing up from some hollow in the ground, walked toward them.

"Had an accident?" he asked, in what he evidently meant for a friendly voice.

"A little one, easily mended," Tom answered.

He was about to take off his goggles, but at sight of the man's face a change came over the countenance of Tom Swift, and he replaced the eye protectors. Then Tom turned to Mr. Damon, as if to ask a question, but the stranger came so close, evidently curious to see the aircraft at close quarters, that the young inventor could not speak without being overheard.

Tom got out his kit of tools to repair the broken control, and the man watched him curiously. As he tinkered away, something was stirring among the past memories of the inventor. A question he asked himself over and over again was:

"Where have I seen this man before? His face is familiar, but I can't place him. He is associated with something unpleasant. But where have I seen this man before?"

Chapter II
Tom's Indifference

"Did you make this machine yourself?" asked the stranger of Tom, as the young inventor worked at the damaged part of his craft.

Mr. Damon had also alighted, taken off his goggles, and was looking aloft, where the army aircraft were going through various evolutions, and down below, where the young soldiers were drilling under such conditions, as far as possible, as they might meet with when some of their number went "over the top." Mr. Damon was murmuring to himself such remarks as:

"Bless my fountain pen! look at that chap turning upside down! Bless my inkwell!"

"I beg your pardon," remarked Tom Swift, following the remark of the man, whose face he was trying to recall. It was not that Tom had not heard the question, but he was trying to gain time before answering.

"I asked if you made this machine yourself," went on the man, as he peered about at the Hawk. "It isn't like any I've ever seen before, and I know something about airships. It has some new wrinkles on it, and I thought you might have evolved them yourself. Not that it's an amateur affair, by any means!" he added hastily, as if fearing the young inventor might resent the implication that his machine was a home-made product.

"Yes, I originated this," answered Tom, as he put a new turn-buckle in place; "but I didn't actually construct it—that is, except for some small parts. It was made in the shop—"

"Over at the army construction plant, I presume," interrupted the man quickly, as he motioned toward the big factory, not far from Shopton, where aircraft for Uncle Sam's Army were being turned out by the hundreds.

"Might as well let him think that," mused Tom; "at least until I can figure out who he is and what he wants."

"This is different from most of those up there," and the stranger pointed toward the circling craft on high. "A bit more speedy, I guess, isn't it?"

"Well, yes, in a way," agreed Tom, who was bending over his craft. He stole a side look at the man. The face was becoming more and more familiar, yet something about it puzzled Tom Swift.

"I've seen him before, and yet he didn't look like that," thought the young inventor. "It's different, somehow. Now why should my memory play me a trick like this? Who in the world can he be?"

Tom straightened up, and tossed a monkey wrench into the tool box.

"Get everything fixed?" asked the stranger.

"I think so," and the young inventor tried to make his answer pleasant. "It was only a small break, easily fixed."

"Then you'll be on your way again?"

"Yes. Are you ready?" called Tom to Mr. Damon.

"Bless my timetable, yes! I didn't think you'd start back again so soon. There's one young fellow up there who has looped the loop three times, and I expect him to fall any minute."

"Oh, I guess he knows his business," Tom said easily. "We'll be getting back now."

"One moment!" called the man. "I beg your pardon for troubling you, but you seem to be a mechanic, and that's just the sort of man I'm looking for. Are you open to an offer to do some inventive and constructive work?"

Tom was on his guard instantly.

"Well, I can't say that I am," he answered. "I am pretty busy—"

"This would pay well," went on the man eagerly. "I am a stranger around here, but I can furnish satisfactory references. I am in need of a good mechanic, an inventor as well, who can do what you seem to have done so well. I had hopes of getting some one at the army plant."

"I guess they're not letting any of their men go," said Tom, as Mr. Damon climbed to his seat in the Hawk.

"No, I soon found that out. But I thought perhaps you—"

Tom shook his head.

"I'm sorry," he answered, "but I'm otherwise engaged, and very busy."

"One moment!" called the man, as he saw Tom about to start "Is the Swift Company plant far from here?"

Tom felt something like a thrill go through him. There was an unexpected note in the man's voice. The face of the young inventor lightened, and the doubts melted away.

"No, it isn't far," Tom answered, shouting to be heard above the crackling bangs of the motor. And then, as the craft soared into the air, he cried exultingly:

"I have it! I know who he is! The scoundrel! His beard fooled me, and he probably didn't know me with these goggles on. But now I know him!"

"Bless my calendar!" cried Mr. Damon. "What are you talking about?"

But Tom did not answer, for the reason that just then the Hawk fell into an "air pocket," and needed all his attention to straighten her out and get her on a level course again.

And while Tom Swift is thus engaged in speeding his aircraft along the upper regions toward his home, it will take but a few moments to acquaint my new readers with something of the history of the young inventor. Those who have read the previous books in this series need be told nothing about our hero.

Tom Swift was an inventor of note, as was his father. Mr. Swift was now quite aged and not in robust health, but he was active at times and often aided Tom when some knotty point came up.

Tom and his father lived on the outskirts of the town of Shopton, and near their home were various buildings in which the different machines and appliances were made. Tom's mother was dead, but Mrs. Baggert, the housekeeper, was as careful in looking after Tom and his father as any woman could be.

In addition to these three, the household consisted of Eradicate Sampson, an aged colored servant, and, it might almost be added, his mule Boomerang; but Boomerang had manners that, at times, did not make him a welcome addition to any household. Then there was the giant Koku, one of two big men Tom had brought back with him from the land where the young inventor had been held captive for a time.

The first book of this series is called "Tom Swift and His Motor Cycle," and it was in acquiring possession of that machine that Tom met his friend Mr. Wakefield Damon, who lived in a neighboring town. Mr. Damon owned the motor cycle originally, but when it attempted to climb a tree with him he sold it to Tom.

Tom had many adventures on the machine, and it started him on his inventive career. From then on he had had a series of surprising adventures. He had traveled in his motor boat, in an airship, and then had taken to a submarine. In his electric runabout he showed what the speediest car on the road could do, and when he sent his wireless message, the details of which can be found set down in the volume of that name, Tom saved the castaways of Earthquake Island.

Tom Swift had many other thrilling escapes, one from among the diamond makers, and another from the caves of ice; and he made the quickest flight on record in his sky racer.

Tom's wizard camera, his great searchlight, his giant cannon, his photo telephone, his aerial warship and the big tunnel he helped to dig, brought him credit, fame, and not a little money. He had not long been back from an expedition to Honduras, dubbed "the land of wonders," when he was again busy on some of his many ideas. And it was to get some relief from his thoughts that he had taken the flight with Mr. Damon on the day the present story opens.

"What are you so excited about, Tom?" asked his friend, as the Hawk alighted near the shed back of the young inventor's home. "Bless my scarf pin! but any one would think you'd just discovered the true method of squaring the circle."

"Well, it's almost as good as that, and more practical," Tom said, with a smile, as he motioned to Koku to put away the aircraft "I know who that man is, now."

"What man, Tom?"

"The one who was questioning me when I was fixing the airship. I kept puzzling and puzzling as to his identity, and, all at once, it came to me. Do you know who he is, Mr. Damon?"

"No, I can't say that I do, Tom. But, as you say, there was something vaguely familiar about him. It seemed as if I must have seen him before, and yet—"

"That's just the way it struck me. What would you say if I told you that man was Blakeson, of Blakeson and Grinder, the rival tunnel contractors who made such trouble for us?"

"You mean down in Peru, Tom?"

"Yes."

Mr. Damon started in surprise, and then exclaimed:

"Bless my ear mufflers, Tom, but you're right! That was Blakeson! I didn't know him with his beard, but that was Blakeson, all right! Bless my foot-warmer! What do you suppose he is doing around here?"

"I don't know, Mr. Damon, but I'd give a good deal to know. It isn't any good, I'll wager on that. He didn't seem to know me or you, either—unless he did and didn't let on. I suppose it was because of my goggles—and you were gazing up in the air most of the time. I don't think he knew either of us."

"It didn't seem so, Tom. But what is he doing here? Do you think he is working at the army camp, or helping make Liberty Motors for the aircraft that are going to beat the Germans?"

"Hardly. He didn't seem to be connected with the camp. He wanted a mechanic, and hinted that I might do. Jove! if he really didn't know who I was, and finds out, say! won't he be surprised?"

"Rather," agreed Mr Damon. "Well, Tom, I had a nice little ride. And now I must be getting back. But if you contemplate a trip anywhere, don't forget to let me know."

"I don't count on going anywhere soon," Tom answered. "I have something on hand that will occupy all my time, though I don't just like it. However, I'm going to do my best," and he waved good-bye to Mr. Damon, who went off blessing various parts of his anatomy or clothing, an odd habit he had.

As Tom turned to go into the house, the unsettled look still on his face, some one hailed him.

"I say, Tom. Hello! Wait a minute! I've got something to show you!"

"Oh, hello, Ned Newton!" Called back the young inventor. "Well, if it's Liberty Bonds, you don't need to show me any, for dad and I will buy all we can without seeing them."

"I know that, Tom, and it was a dandy subscription you gave me. I didn't come about that, though I may be around the next time Uncle Sam wants the people to dig down in their socks. This is something different," and Ned Newton, a young banker of Shopton and a lifelong friend of Tom's, drew a paper from his pocket as he advanced across the lawn.

"There, Tom Swift!" he cried, flipping out an illustrated page, evidently from some illustrated newspaper. "There's the very latest from the other side. A London banker friend of mine sent it to me, and it got past the censor all right. It's the first authentic photograph of the newest and biggest British tank. Isn't that a wonder?"

Ned held up the paper which had in it a fullpage photograph of a monster tank—those weird machines traveling on endless steel belts of caterpillar construction, armored, riveted and plated, with machine guns bristling here and there.

"Isn't that great, Tom? Can you beat it? It's the most wonderful machine of the age, even counting some of yours. Can you beat it?"

Tom took the paper indifferently, and his manner surprised his chum.

"Well, what's the matter, Tom?" asked Ned. "Don't you think that great? Why don't you say something? You don't mean to say you've seen that picture before?"

"No, Ned."

"Then what's the matter with you? Isn't that wonderful?"

Chapter III Ned is Worried

Tom Swift did not answer for several seconds. He stood holding the paper Ned had given him, the sun slanting on the picture of the big British tank. But the young inventor did not appear to see it. Instead, his eyes were as though contemplating something afar off.

"Well, this gets me!" cried Ned, his voice showing impatience. "Here I go and get a picture of the latest machine the British armies are smashing up the Boches with, and bring it to you fresh from the mail—I even quit my Liberty Bond business to do it, and I know some dandy prospects, too—and here you look at it like a—like a fish!" burst out Ned.

"Say, old man, I guess that's right!" admitted Tom. "I wasn't thinking about it, to tell you the truth."

"Why not?" Ned demanded. "Isn't it great, Tom? Did you ever see anything like it?"

"Yes."

"You did?" Cried Ned, in surprise. "Where? Say, Tom Swift, are you keeping something from me?"

"I mean no, Ned. I never have seen a British tank."

"Well, did you ever see a picture like this before?" Ned persisted.

"No, not exactly like that But—"

"Well, what do you think of it?" cried the young banker, who was giving much of his time to selling bonds for the Government. "Isn't it great?"

Tom considered a moment before replying. Then he said slowly:

"Well, yes, Ned, it is a pretty good machine. But—"

"'But!' Howling tomcats! Say, what's the 'matter with you, anyhow, Tom? This is great! 'But!' 'But me no buts!' This is, without exception, the greatest thing out since an airship. It will win the war for us and the Allies, too, and don't you forget it! Fritz's barbed wire and dugouts and machine gun emplacements can't stand for a minute against these tanks! Why, Tom, they can crawl on their back as well as any other way, and they don't mind a shower of shrapnel or a burst of machine gun lead, any more than an alligator minds a swarm of gnats. The only thing that makes 'em hesitate a bit is a Jack Johnson or a Bertha shell, and it's got to be a pretty big one, and in the right place, to do much damage. These tanks are great, and there's nothing like 'em."

"Oh, yes there is, Ned!"

"There is!" cried Ned. "What do you mean?"

"I mean there may be something like them—soon."

"There may? Say, Tom—"

"Now don't ask me a lot of questions, Ned, for I can't answer them. When I say there may be something like them, I mean it isn't beyond the realms of possibility that some one—perhaps the Germans—may turn out even bigger and better tanks."

"Oh!" And Ned's voice showed his disappointment. "I thought maybe you were in on that game yourself, Tom. Say, couldn't you get up something almost as good as this?" and he indicated the picture in the paper. "Isn't that wonderful?"

"Oh, well, it's good, Ned, but there are others. Yes, Dad, I'm coming," he called, as he saw his father beckoning to him from a distant building.

"Well, I've got to get along," said Ned. "But I certainly am disappointed, Tom. I thought you'd go into a fit over this picture—it's one of the first allowed to get out of England, my London friend said. And instead of enthusing you're as cold as a clam;" and Ned shook his head in puzzled and disappointed fashion as he walked slowly along beside the young inventor.

They passed a new building, one of the largest in the group of the many comprising the Swift plant. Ned looked at the door which bore a notice to the effect that no one was admitted unless bearing a special permit, or accompanied by Mr. Swift or Tom.

"What's this, Tom?" asked Ned. "Some new wrinkle?"

"Yes, an invention I'm working on. It isn't in shape yet to be seen."

"It must be something big, Tom," observed Ned, as he viewed the large building.

"It is."

"And say, what a whopping big fence you've got around the back yard!" went on the young banker. "Looks like a baseball field, but it would take some scrambling on the part of a back-lots kid to get over it."

"That's what it's for—to keep people out."

"I see! Well, I've got to get along. I'm a bit back in my day's quota of selling Liberty Bonds, and I've got to hustle. I'm sorry I bothered you about that tank picture, Tom."

"Oh, it wasn't a bother—don't think that for a minute, Ned! I was glad to see it."

"Well, he didn't seem so, and his manner was certainly queer," mused Ned, as he walked away, and turned in time to see Tom enter the new building, which had such a high fence all around it. "I never saw him more indifferent. I wonder if Tom isn't interested in seeing Uncle Sam help win this war? That's the way it struck me. I thought surely Tom would go up in the air, and say this was a dandy," and Ned unfolded the paper and took another look at the British tank photograph. "If there's anything can beat that I'd like to see it," he mused.

"But I suppose Tom has discovered some new kind of air stabilizer, or a different kind of carburetor that will vaporize kerosene as well as gasolene. If he has, why doesn't he offer it to Uncle Sam? I wonder if Tom is pro-German? No, of Course he can't be!" and Ned laughed at his own idea.

"At the same time, it is queer," he mused on. "There is something wrong with Tom Swift."

Once more Ned looked at the picture. It was a representation of one of the newest and largest of the British tanks. In appearance these are not unlike great tanks, though they are neither round nor square, being shaped, in fact, like two wedges with the broad ends put together, and the sharper ends sticking out, though there is no sharpness to a tank, the "noses" both being blunt.

Around each outer edge runs an endless belt of steel plates, hinged together, with ridges at the joints, and these broad belts of steel plates, like the platforms of some moving stairways used in department stores, moving around, give motion to the tank.

Inside, well protected from the fire of enemy guns by steel plates, are the engines for driving the belts, or caterpillar wheels, as they are called. There is also the steering apparatus, and the guns that fire on the enemy. There are cramped living and sleeping quarters for the tank's crew, more limited than those of a submarine.

The tank is ponderous, the smallest of them, which were those first constructed, weighing forty-two tons, or about as much as a good-sized railroad freight car. And it is this ponderosity, with its slow but resistless movement, that gives the tank its power.

The tank, by means of the endless belts of steel plates, can travel over the roughest country. It can butt into a tree, a stone wall, or a house, knock over the obstruction, mount it, crawl over it, and slide down into a hole on the other side and crawl out again, on the level, or at an angle. Even if overturned, the tanks can sometimes right themselves and keep on. At the rear are trailer wheels, partly used in steering and partly for reaching over gaps or getting out of holes. The tanks can turn in their own length, by moving one belt in one direction and the other oppositely.

Inside there is nothing much but machinery of the gasolene type, and the machine guns. The tank is closed except for small openings out of which the guns project, and slots through which the men inside look out to guide themselves or direct their fire.

Such, in brief, is a British tank, one of the most powerful and effective weapons yet loosed against the Germans. They are useful in tearing down the barbed-wire entanglements on the Boche side of No Man's Land, and they can clear the way up to and past the trenches, which they can straddle and wriggle across like some giant worm.

"And to think that Tom Swift didn't enthuse over these!" murmured Ned. "I wonder what's the matter with him!"

Chapter IV
Queer Doings

There was a subdued air of activity about the Swift plant. Subdued, owing to the fact that it was mostly confined to one building—the new, large one, about which stretched a high and strong fence, made with tongue-and-groove boards so that no prying eyes might find a crack, even, through which to peer.

In and out of the other buildings the workmen went as they pleased, though there were not many of them, for Tom and his father were devoting most of their time and energies to what was taking place in the big, new structure. But here there was an entirely different procedure.

Workmen went in and out, to be sure, but each time they emerged they were scrutinized carefully, and when they went in they had to exhibit their passes to a man on guard at the single entrance; and the passes were not scrutinized perfunctorily, either.

Near the building, about which there seemed to be an air of mystery, one day, a week after the events narrated in the opening chapters, strolled the giant Koku. Not far away, raking up a pile of refuse, was Eradicate Sampson, the aged colored man of all work. Eradicate approached nearer and nearer the entrance to the building, pursuing his task of gathering up leaves, dirt and sticks with the teeth of his rake. Then Koku, who had been lounging on a bench in the shade of a tree, Called:

"No more, Eradicate!"

"No mo' whut?" asked the negro quickly. "I didn't axt yo' fo' nuffin yit!"

"No more come here!" said the giant, pointing to the building and speaking English with an evident effort. "Master say no one come too close."

"Huh! He didn't go fo' t' mean me!" exclaimed Eradicate. "I kin go anywheres; I kin!"

"Not here!" and Koku interposed his giant frame between the old man and the first step leading into the secret building. "You no come in here."

"Who say so?"

"Me—I say so! I on guard. I what you call special policeman—detectiff—no let enemies in!"

"Huh! You's a hot deteckertiff, yo' is!" snorted Eradicate. "Anyhow, dem orders don't mean me! I kin go anywhere, I kin!"

"Not here!" said Koku firmly. "Master Tom say let nobody come near but workmen who have got writing-paper. You no got!"

"No, but I kin git one, an' I's gwine t' hab it soon! I'll see Massa Tom, dat's whut I will. I guess yo' ain't de only deckertiff on de place. I kin go on guard, too!" and Eradicate, dropping his rake, strolled away in his temper to seek the young inventor.

"Well, Rad, what is it?" asked Tom, as he met the colored man. The young inventor was on his way to the mysterious shop. "What is troubling you?"

"It's dat dar giant. He done says as how he's on guard—a deteckertiff—an' I can't go nigh dat buildin' t' sweep up de refuse."

"Well, that's right, Rad. I'd prefer that you keep away. I'm doing some special work in there and it's—"

"Am it dangerous, Massa Tom? I ain't askeered! Anybody whut kin drive mah mule Boomerang—"

"I know, Eradicate, but this isn't so dangerous. It's just secret, and I don't want too many people about. You can go anywhere else except there. Koku is on guard."

"Den can't I be, Massa Tom?" asked the colored man eagerly. "I kin guard an' detect same as dat low-down, good-fo'-nuffin white trash Koku!"

Tom hesitated.

"I suppose I could get you a sort of officer's badge," he mused, half aloud.

"Dat's whut I want!" eagerly exclaimed Eradicate. "I ain't gwine hab dat Koku—dat cocoanut—crowin' ober me! I kin guard an' detect as good's anybody!"

And the upshot of it was that Eradicate was given a badge, and put on a special post, far enough from Koku to keep the two from quarreling, and where, even if he failed in keeping a proper lookout, the old servant could do no harm by his oversight.

"It'll please him, and won't hurt us," said Tom to his father. "Koku will keep out any prying persons."

"I suppose you are doing well to keep it a secret, Tom," said Mr. Swift, "but it seems as if you might announce it soon."

"Perhaps we may, Dad, if all goes well. I've given her a partial shop-tryout, and she works well. But there is still plenty to do. Did I tell you about meeting Blakeson?"

"Yes, and I can't understand why he should be in this vicinity. Do you think he has had any intimation of what you are doing?"

"It's hard to say, and yet I would not be surprised. When Uncle Sam couldn't keep secret the fact of our first soldiers sailing for France. How can I expect to keep this secret? But they won't get any details until I'm ready, I'm sure of that."

"Koku is a good discourager," said Mr. Swift, with a chuckle. "You couldn't have a better guard, Tom."

"No, and if I can keep him and Eradicate from trying to pull off rival detective stunts, or 'deteckertiff,' as Rad calls it, I'll be all right. Now let's have another go at that carburetor. There's our weak point, for it's getting harder and harder all the while to get high-grade gasolene, and we'll have to come to alcohol of low proof, or kerosene, I'm thinking."

"I wouldn't be surprised, Tom. Well, perhaps we can get up a new style of carburetor that will do the trick. Now look at this needle valve; I've given it a new turn," and father and son went into technical details connected with their latest invention.

These were busy days at the Swift plant. Men came and went—men with queerly shaped parcels frequently—and they were admitted to the big new building after first passing Eradicate and then Koku, and it would be hard to say which guard was the more careful. Only, of course, Koku had the final decision, and more than one person was turned back after Eradicate had passed him, much to the disgust of the negro.

"Pooh! Dat giant don't know a workman when he sees 'im!" snorted Eradicate. "He so lazy his own se'f dat he don't know a workman! Ef I sees a spy, Massa Tom, or a crook, I's gwine git him, suah pop!"

"I hope you do, Rad. We can't afford to let this secret get out," said the young inventor.

It was one evening, when taking a short cut to his home, that Mr. Nestor, the father of Mary Nestor, in whom Tom was more than ordinarily interested, passed not far from the big enclosure which was guarded, on the factory side, day and night. Inside, though out of sight and hidden by the high fence, were other guards.

As Mr. Nestor passed along the fence, rather vaguely wondering why it was so high, tight and strong, he felt the ground trembling beneath his feet. It rumbled and shook as though a distant train were passing, and yet there was none due now, for Mr. Nestor had just left one, and another would not arrive for an hour.

"That's queer," mused Mary's father. "If I didn't know to the contrary, I'd say that sounded like heavy guns being fired from a distance, or else blasting. It seems to come from the Swift place," he went on. "I wonder what they're up to in there."

Suddenly the rumbling became more pronounced, and mingled with it, in the dusk of the evening, were the shouts of men.

"Look out!" some one cried. "She's going for the fence!"

A second later there was a cracking and straining of boards, and the fence near Mr. Nestor bulged out as though something big, powerful and mighty were pressing it from the inner side.

But the fence held, or else the pressure was removed, for the bulge went back into place, though some of the boards were splintered.

"Have to patch that up in the morning," called another voice, and Mr. Nestor recognized it as that of Tom Swift.

"What queer doings are going on here?" mused Mary's father. "Have they got a wild bull shut up in there, and is he trying to get out? Lucky for me he didn't," and he hurried on, the rumbling noise become fainter until it died away altogether.

That night, after his supper and while reading the paper and smoking a cigar, Mr. Nestor spoke to his daughter.

"Mary, have you seen anything of Tom Swift lately?"

"Why, yes, Father. He was over for a little while the other night, but he didn't stay long. Why do you ask?"

"Oh, nothing special. I just came past his place and I heard some queer noises, that's all. He's up to some more of his tricks, I guess. Has be enlisted yet?"

"No.

"Is he going to?"

"I don't know," and Mary seemed a bit put out by this simple question. "What do you mean by his tricks?" she asked, and a close observer might have thought she was anxious to get away from the subject of Tom's enlistment.

"Oh, like that one when he sent you something in a box labeled 'dynamite,' and gave us all a scare. You can't tell what Tom Swift is going to do next. He's up to something now, I'll wager, and I don't believe any good will come of it."

"You didn't think so after he sent his wireless message, and saved us from Earthquake Island," said Mary, smiling.

"Hum! Well, that was different," snapped Mr. Nestor. "This time I'm sure he's up to some nonsense! The idea of crashing down a fence! Why doesn't he enlist like the other chaps, or sell Liberty Bonds like Ned Newton?" and Mr. Nestor looked sharply at his daughter. "Ned gave up a big salary as the Swifts financial man—a place he had held for a year—to go back to the bank for less, just so he could help the Government in the financial end of this war. Is Tom doing as much for his country?"

"I'm sure I don't know," answered Mary; and soon after, with averted face, she left the room.

"Hum! Queer goings on," mused Mr. Nestor. "Tom Swift may be all right, but he's got an unbalanced streak in him that will bear looking out for, that's what I think!"

And having settled this matter, at least to his own satisfaction, Mr. Nestor resumed his smoking and reading.

A little later the bell rang. There was a murmur of voices in the hall, and Mr. Nestor, half listening, heard a voice he knew.

"There's Tom Swift now!" he exclaimed. "I'm going to find out why he doesn't enlist!"

Chapter V
"Is He a Slacker?"

Mr. Nestor, whatever else he was, proved to be a prudent father. He did not immediately go into the front room, whither Mary and Tom hastened, their voices mingling in talk and laughter.

Mr. Nestor, after leaving the young folks alone for a while, with a loud "Ahem!" and a rattling of his paper as he laid it aside, started for the parlor.

"Good-evening, Mr. Nestor!" said Tom, rising to shake hands with the father of his young and pretty hostess.

"Hello, Tom!" was the cordial greeting, in return. "What's going on up at your place?" went on Mr. Nestor, as he took a chair.

"Oh, nothing very special," Tom answered. "We're turning out different kinds of machines as usual, and dad and I are experimenting, also as usual."

"I suppose so. But what nearly broke the fence to-night?"

Tom started, and looked quickly at his host.

"Were you there?" he asked quickly.

"Well, I happened to be passing—took a short cut home—and I heard some queer goings on at your place. I was speaking to Mary about them, and wondering—"

"Father, perhaps Tom doesn't want to talk about his inventions," interrupted Mary. "You know some of them are secret—"

"Oh, I wasn't exactly asking for information!" exclaimed Mr. Nestor quickly. "I just happened to hear the fence crash, and I was wondering if something was coming out at me. Didn't know but what that giant of yours was on a rampage, Tom," and he laughed.

"No, it wasn't anything like that," and Tom's voice was more sober than the occasion seemed to warrant. "It was one of our new machines, and it didn't act just right. No great damage was done, though. How do you find business, Mr. Nestor, since the war spirit has grown stronger?" asked Tom, and it seemed to both Mary and her father that the young inventor deliberately changed the subject.

"Well, it isn't all it might be," said the other. "It's hard to get good help. A lot of our boys enlisted, and some were taken in the draft. By the way, Tom, have they called on you yet?"

"No. Not yet."

"You didn't enlist?"

"Ned Newton tried to," broke in Mary, "but the quota for this locality was filled, and they told him he'd better wait for the draft. He wouldn't do that and tried again. Then the bank people heard about it and had him exempted. They said he was too valuable to them, and he has been doing remarkably well in selling Liberty Bonds!" and Mary's eyes sparkled with her emotions.

"Yes, Ned is a crackerjack salesman!" agreed Tom, no less enthusiastically. "He's sold more bonds, in proportion, for his bank, than any other in this county. Dad and I both took some, and have promised him more. I am glad now that we let him go, although we valued his services highly. We hope to have him back later."

"He can put me down for more bonds too!" said Mr. Nestor. "I'm going to see Germany beaten if it takes every last dollar I have!"

"That's what I say!" Cried Mary. "I took out all my savings, except a little I'm keeping to buy a wedding present for Jennie Morse. Did you know she was going to get married, Tom?" she asked.

"I heard so."

"Well, all but what I want for a wedding present to her has gone into Liberty Bonds. Isn't this a history-making time, Tom?"

"Indeed it is, Mary!"

"Everybody who has a part in it—whether he fights as a soldier or only knits like the Red Cross girls—will be telling about it for years after," went on the girl, and she looked at Tom eagerly.

"Yes," he agreed. "These are queer times. We don't know exactly where we're at. A lot of our men have been called. We tried to have some of them exempted, and did manage it in a few cases."

"You did?" cried Mr. Nestor, as if in surprise. "You stopped men from going to war!"

"Only so they could work on airship motors for the Government," Tom quietly explained.

"Oh! Well, of course, that's part of the game," agreed Mary's father. "A lot more of our boys are going off next week. Doesn't it make you thrill, Tom, when you see them marching off, even if they haven't their uniforms yet? Jove, if I wasn't too old, I'd go in a minute!"

"Father!" cried Mary.

"Yes, I would!" he declared. "The German government has got to be beaten, and we've got to do our bit; everybody has—man, woman and child!"

"Yes," agreed Tom, in a low voice, "that's very true. But every one, in a sense, has to judge for himself what the 'bit' is. We can't all do the same."

There was a little silence, and then Mary went over to the piano and played. It was a rather welcome relief, under the circumstances, from the conversation.

"Mary, what do you think of Tom?" asked Mr. Nestor, when the visitor had gone.

"What do I think of him?" And she blushed.

"I mean about his not enlisting. Do you think he's a slacker?"

"A slacker? Why, Father!"

"Oh, I don't mean he's afraid. We've seen proof enough of his courage, and all that. But I mean don't you think he wants stirring up a bit?"

"He is going to Washington to-morrow, Father. He told me so to-night. And it may be—"

"Oh, well, then maybe it's all right," hastily said Mr. Nestor. "He may be going to get a commission in the engineer corps. It isn't like Tom Swift to hang back, and yet it does begin to look as though he cared more for his queer inventions—machines that butt down fences than for helping Uncle Sam. But I'll reserve judgment."

"You'd better, Father!" and Mary laughed—a little. Yet there was a worried look on her face.

During the next few nights Mr. Nestor made it a habit to take the short cut from the railroad station, coming past the big fence that enclosed one particular building of the Swift plant.

"I wonder if there's a hole where I could look through," said Mr. Nestor to himself. "Of course I don't believe in spying on what another man is doing, and yet I'm too good a friend of Tom's to want to see him make a fool of himself. He ought to be in the army, or helping Uncle Sam in some way. And yet if he spends all his time on some foolish contraption, like a new kind of traction plow, what good is that? If I could get a glimpse of it, I might drop a friendly hint in his ear."

But there were no cracks in the fence, or, if there were, it was too dark to see them, and also too dark to behold anything on the other side of the barrier. So Mr. Nestor, wondering much, kept on his way.

It was a day or so after this that Ned Newton paid a visit to the Swift home. Mr. Swift was not in the house, being out in one of the various buildings, Mrs. Baggert said.

"Where's Tom?" asked the bond salesman.

"Oh, he hasn't come back from Washington yet," answered the housekeeper.

"He is making a long stay."

"Yes, he went about a week ago on some business. But we expect him back to-day."

"Well, then I'll see him. I called to ask if Mr. Swift didn't want to take a few more bonds. We want to double our allotment for Shopton, and beat out some of the other towns in this section. I'll go to see Mr. Swift."

On his way to find Tom's father Ned passed the big building in front of which Eradicate and Koku were on guard. They nodded to Ned, who passed them, wondering much as to what it was Tom was so secretive about.

"It's the first time I remember when he worked on an invention without telling me something about it," mused Ned. "Well, I suppose it will all come out in good time. Anything new, Rad?"

"No, Massa Ned, nuffin much. I'm detectin' around heah; keepin' Dutchmen spies away!"

"And Koku is helping you, I suppose?"

"Whut, him? Dat big, good-fo'-nuffin white trash? No, sah! I's detectin' by mahse'f, dat's whut I is!" and Eradicate strutted proudly up and down on his allotted part of the beat, being careful not to approach the building too closely, for that was Koku's ground.

Ned smiled, and passed on. He found Mr. Swift, secured his subscription to more bonds, and was about to leave when he heard a call down the road and saw Tom coming in his small racing car, which had been taken to the depot by one of the workmen.

"Hello, old man!" cried Ned affectionately, as his chum alighted with a jump. "Where have you been?"

"Down to Washington. Had a bit of a chat with the President and gave him some of my views."

"About the war, I suppose?" laughed Ned.

"Yes."

"Did you get your commission?"

"Commission?" And there was a wondering look on Tom's face.

"Yes. Mary Nestor said she thought maybe you were going to Washington to take an examination for the engineering corps or something like that. Did you get made an officer?"

"No," answered Tom slowly. "I went to Washington to get exempted."

"Exempted?" Cried Ned, and his voice sounded strained.

Chapter VI
Seeing Things

For a moment Tom Swift looked at his chum. Then something of what was passing in the mind of the young bond salesman must have been reflected to Tom, for he said,

"Look here, old man; I know it may seem a bit strange to go to all that trouble to get exempted from the draft, to which I am eligible, but, believe me, there's a reason. I can't say anything now, but I'll tell you as soon as I can—tell everybody, in fact. Just now it isn't in shape to talk about."

"Oh, that's all right, Tom," and Ned tried to make his voice sound natural. "I was just wondering, that's all. I wanted to go to the front the worst way, but they wouldn't let me. I was sort of hoping you could, and come back to tell me about it."

"I may yet, Ned."

"You may? Why, I thought—"

"Oh, I'm only exempted for a time. I've got certain things to do, and I couldn't do 'em if I enlisted or was drafted. So I've been excused for a time. Now I've got a pile of work to do. What are you up to Ned? Same old story?"

"Liberty Bonds—yes. Your father just took some more."

"And so will I, Ned. I can do that, anyhow, even if I don't enlist. Put me down for another two thousand dollars' worth."

"Say, Tom, that's fine! That will make my share bigger than I counted on. Shopton will beat the record."

"That's good. We ought to pull strong and hearty for our home town. How's everything else?"

"Oh, so-so. I see Koku and Eradicate trying to outdo one another in guarding that part of your plant," and Ned nodded toward the big new building.

"Yes, I had to let Rad play detective. Not that he can do anything—he's too old. But it keeps him and Koku from quarreling all the while. I've got to be pretty careful about that shop. It's got a secret in it that—Well, the less said about it the better."

"You're getting my curiosity aroused, Tom," remarked Ned.

"It'll have to go unsatisfied for a while. Wait a bit and I'll give you a ride. I've got to go over to Sackett on business, and if you're going that way I'll take you."

"What in?"

"The Hawk."

"That's me!" cried Ned. "I haven't been in an aircraft for some time."

"Tell Miles to run her out," requested Tom. "I've got to go in and say hello to dad a minute, and then I'll be with you."

"Seems like something was in the wind, Tom—big doings?" hinted Ned.

"Yes, maybe there is. It all depends on how she turns out."

"You might be speaking of the Hawk or—Mary Nestor!" said Ned, with a sidelong look at his chum.

"As it happens, it's neither one," said Tom, and then he hastened away, to return shortly and guide his fleet little airship, the Hawk, on her aerial journey.

From then on, at least for some time, neither Tom nor Ned mentioned the matters they had been discussing—Tom's failure to enlist, his exemption, and what was being built in the closely guarded shop.

Tom's business in Sackett did not take him long, and then he and Ned went for a little ride in the air.

"It's like old times!" exclaimed Ned, his eyes shining, though Tom could not see them for two reasons. One was that Ned was sitting behind him, and the other was that Ned wore heavy goggles, as did the young pilot. Also, they had to carry on their talk through the speaking tube arrangement.

"Yes, it is a bit like old times," agreed Tom. "We've had some great old experiences together, Ned, haven't we?"

"We surely have! I wonder if we'll have any more? When we were in the submarine, and in your big airship. Say, that big one is the one I always liked! I like big things."

"Do you?" asked Tom. "Well, maybe, when I get—"

But Tom did not finish, for the Hawk unexpectedly poked her nose into an empty pocket in the air just then, and needed a firm hand on the controls. Furthermore, Tom decided against making the confidence that was on the tip of his tongue.

At last the aircraft was straightened out and the pilot guided her on toward the army encampment.

"That's the place I'd like to be," called Ned through the tube as the faint, sweet notes of a bugle floated up from the parade ground.

"Yes, it would be great," admitted Tom. "But there are other things to do for Uncle Sam besides wearing khaki."

"Tom's up to some game," mused Ned. "I mustn't judge him too hastily, or I might make a mistake. And Mary mustn't, either. I'll tell her so."

For Mary Nestor had spoken to Ned concerning Tom, and the curiously secretive air about certain of his activities. And the girl, moreover, had spoken rather coldly of her friend. Ned did not like this. It was not like Mary and Tom to be at odds.

Once more the Hawk came to the ground, this time near the airship sheds adjoining the Swift works. Just as Tom and Ned alighted, one of the workmen summoned the young inventor toward the shop, which was so closely guarded by Koku and Eradicate on the outside.

"I'll have to leave you, Ned," remarked Tom, as he turned away from his chum. "There's a conference on about a new invention."

"Oh, that's all right. Business is business, you know. I've got some bond calls to make myself. I'll see you later."

"Oh, by the way, Ned!" exclaimed Tom, turning back for a moment, "I met an old friend the other day; or rather an old enemy."

"Hum! When you spoke first, I thought you might mean Professor Swyington Bumper, that delightful scientist," remarked Ned. "But he surely was no enemy."

"No; but I meant some one I met about the same time. I met Blakeson, one of the rival contractors when I helped dig the big tunnel."

"Is that so? Where'd you meet him?"

"Right around here. It was certainly a surprise, and at first I couldn't place him. Then the memory of his face came back to me," and Tom related the incident which had taken place the day he and Mr. Damon were out in the Hawk.

"What's he doing around here?" asked Ned.

"That's more than I can say," Tom answered.

"Up to no good, I'll wager!"

"I agree with you," came from Tom. "But I'm on the watch."

"That's wise, Tom. Well, I'll see you later."

During the week which followed this talk Ned was very busy on Liberty Bond work, and, he made no doubt, his chum was engaged also. This prevented them from meeting, but finally Ned, one evening, decided to walk over to the Swift home.

"I'll pay Tom a bit of a call," he mused. "Maybe he'll feel more like talking now. Some of the boys are asking why he doesn't enlist, and maybe if I tell him that he'll make some explanation that will quiet things down a bit. It's a shame that Tom should be talked about."

With this intention in view, Ned kept on toward his chum's house, and he was about to turn in through a small grove of trees, which would lead to a path across the fields, when the young bond salesman was surprised to hear some one running toward him. He could see no one, for the path wound in and out among the trees, but the noise was plain.

"Some one in a hurry," mused Ned.

A moment later he caught sight of a small lad named Harry Telford running toward him. The boy had his hat in his hand, and was speeding through the fast-gathering darkness as though some one were after him.

"What's the rush?" asked Ned. "Playing cops and robbers?" That was a game Tom and Ned had enjoyed in their younger days.

"I—I'm runnin' away!" panted Harry. "I—I seen something!"

"You saw something?" repeated Ned. "What was it—a ghost?" and he laughed, thinking the boy would do the same.

"No, it wasn't no ghost!" declared Harry, casting a look over his shoulder. "It was a wild elephant that I saw, and it's down in a big yard with a fence around it."

"Where's that?" asked Ned. "The circus hasn't come to town this evening, has it?"

"No," answered Harry, "it wasn't no circus. I saw this elephant down in the big yard back of one of Mr. Swift's factories."

"Oh, down there, was it!" exclaimed Ned. "What was it like?"

"Well, I was walking along the top of the hill," explained Harry, "and there's one place where, if you climb a tree, you can look right down in the big fenced-in yard. I guess I'm about the only one that knows about it."

"I don't believe Tom does," mused Ned, "or he'd have had that tree cut down. He doesn't want any spying, I take it. Well, what'd you see?" he asked Harry aloud.

"Saw an elephant, I tell you!", insisted the younger boy. "I was in the tree, looking down, for a lot of us kids has tried to peek through the fence and couldn't I wanted to see what was there."

"And did you?" asked Ned.

"I sure did! And it scared me, too," admitted Harry. "All at once, when I was lookin', I saw the big doors at the back of the shed open, and the elephant waddled out."

"Are you sure you weren't 'seeing things,' like the little boy in the story?" asked Ned.

"Well, I sure did see something!" insisted Harry. "It was a great big gray thing, bigger'n any elephant I ever saw in any circus. It didn't seem to have any tail or trunk, or even legs, but it went slow, just like an elephant does, and it shook the ground, it stepped so hard!"

"Nonsense!" cried Ned.

"Sure I saw it!" cried Harry. "Anyhow," he added, after a moment's thought, "it was as big as an elephant, though not like any I ever saw."

"What did it do?" asked Ned.

"Well, it moved around and then it started for the fence nearest me, where I was up in the tree. I thought it might have seen me, even though it was gettin' dark, and it might bust through; so I ran!"

"Hum! Well, you surely were seeing things," murmured Ned, but, while he made light of what the boy told him, the young bank clerk was thinking: "What is Tom up to now?"

Chapter VII
Up a Tree

"Want to come and have a look?" asked Harry, as Ned paused in the patch of woods, which were in deeper darkness than the rest of the countryside, for night was fast falling.

"Have a look at what?" asked Ned, who was thinking many thoughts just then.

"At the elephant I saw back of the Swift factory. I wouldn't be skeered if you came along."

"Well, I'm going over to see Tom Swift, anyhow," answered Ned, "so I'll walk that way. You can come if you like. I don't care about spying on other people's property—"

"I wasn't spyin'!" exclaimed Harry quickly. "I just happened to look. And then I seen something."

"Well, come on," suggested Ned. "If there's anything there, we'll have a peep at it."

His idea was not to try to see what Tom was evidently endeavoring to conceal, but it was to observe whence Harry had made his observation, and be in a position to tell Tom to guard against unexpected lookers-on from that direction.

During the walk back along the course over which Harry had run so rapidly a little while before, Ned and the boy talked of what the latter had seen.

"Do you think it could be some new kind of elephant?" asked Harry. "You know Tom Swift brought back a big giant from one of his trips, and maybe he's got a bigger elephant than any one ever saw before."

"Nonsense!" laughed Ned. "In the first place, Tom hasn't been on any trip, of late, except to Washington, and the only kind of elephants there are white ones."

"Really?" asked Harry.

"No, that was a joke," explained Ned. "Anyhow, Tom hasn't any giant elephants concealed up his sleeve, I'm sure of that."

"But what could this be?" asked Harry. "It moved just like some big animal."

"Probably some piece of machinery Tom was having carted from one shop to another," went on the young bank clerk. "Most likely he had it covered with a big piece of canvas to keep off the dew, and it was that you saw."

"No, it wasn't!" insisted Harry, but he could not give any further details of what he had seen so that Ned could recognize it. They kept on until they reached the hill, at the bottom of which was the Swift home and the grounds on which the various shops were erected.

"Here's the place where you can look down right into the yard with the high fence around it," explained Harry, as he indicated the spot.

"I can't see anything."

"You have to climb up the tree," Harry went on. "Here, this is the one, and he indicated a stunted and gnarled pine, the green branches of which would effectually screen any one who once got in it a few feet above the ground.

"Well, I may as well have a look," decided Ned. "It can't do Tom any harm, and it may be of some service to him. Here goes!"

Up into the tree he scrambled, not without some difficulty, for the branches were close together and stiff, and Ned tore his coat in the effort. But he finally got a position where, to his surprise, he could look down into the very enclosure from which Tom was so particular to keep prying eyes.

"You can see right down in it!" Ned exclaimed.

"I told you so," returned Harry. "But do you see—it?"

Ned looked long and carefully. It was lighter, now that they were out of the clump of woods, and he had the advantage of having the last glow of the sunset at his back. Even with that it was difficult to make out objects on the surface of the enclosed field some hundred or more feet below.

"Do you see anything?" asked Harry again.

"No, I can't say I do," Ned answered. "The place seems to be deserted."

"Well, there was something there," insisted Harry. "Maybe you aren't lookin' at the right place."

"Have a look yourself, then," suggested Ned, as he got down, a task no more to his liking than the climb upward had been.

Harry made easier work of it, being smaller and more used to climbing trees, a luxury Ned had, perforce, denied himself since going to work in the bank.

Harry peered about, and then, with a sigh that had in it somewhat of disappointment, said:

"No; there's nothing there now. But I did see something."

"Are you sure?" asked Ned.

"Positive!" asserted the other.

"Well, whatever it was—some bit of machinery he was moving, I fancy— Tom has taken it in now," remarked Ned. "Better not say anything about this, Harry. Tom mightn't like it known."

"No, I won't."

"And don't come here again to look. I know you like to see strange things, but if you'll wait I'll ask Tom, as soon as it's ready, to let you have a closer view of whatever it was you saw. Better keep away from this tree."

"I will," promised the younger lad. "But I'd like to know what it was—if it really was a giant elephant Say! if a fellow had a troop of them he could have a lot of fun with 'em, couldn't he?"

"How?" asked Ned, hardly conscious of what his companion was saying.

"Why, he could dress 'em up in coats of mail, like the old knights used to wear, and turn 'em loose against the Germans. Think of a regiment of elephants, wearin' armor plates like a battleship, carryin' on their backs a lot of soldiers with machine guns and chargin' against Fritz! Cracky, that would be a sight!"

"I should say so!" agreed Ned, with a laugh. "There's nothing the matter with your imagination, Harry, my boy!"

"And maybe that's what Tom's doin'!"

"What do you mean?"

"I mean maybe he is trainin' elephants to fight in the war. You know he made an aerial warship, so why couldn't he have a lot of armor plated elephants?"

"Oh, I suppose he could if he wanted to," admitted Ned. "But I guess he isn't doing that. Don't get to going too fast in high speed, Harry, or you may have nightmare. Well, I'm going down to see Tom."

"And you won't tell him I was peekin'?"

"Not if you don't do it again. I'll advise him to have that tree cut down, though. It's too good a vantage spot."

Harry turned and went in the direction of his home, while Ned kept on down the hill toward the house of his chum. The young bond salesman was thinking of many things as he tramped, along, and among them was the information Harry had just given.

But Ned did not pay a visit to his chum that evening. When he reached the house he found that Tom had gone out, leaving no word as to when he would be back.

"Oh, well, I can tell him to-morrow," thought Ned.

It was not, however, until two days later that Ned found the time to visit Tom again. On this occasion, as before, he took the road through the clump of woods where he had seen Harry running.

"And while I'm about it," mused Ned, "I may as well go on to the place where the tree stands and make sure, by daylight, what I only partially surmised in the evening—that Tom's place can be looked down on from that vantage point."

Sauntering slowly along, for he was in no special hurry, having the remainder of the day to himself, Ned approached the hill where the tree stood from which Harry had said he had seen what he took to be a giant elephant, perhaps in armor.

"It's a good clear day," observed Ned, "and fine for seeing. I wonder if I'll be able to see anything."

It was necessary first to ascend the hill to a point where it overhung, in a measure, the Swift property, though the holdings of Tom and his father were some distance beyond the eminence. The tree from which Ned and Harry had made their observations was on a knob of the hill, the stunted pine standing out from among others like it.

"Well, here goes for another torn coat," grimly observed Ned, as he prepared to climb. "But I'll be more careful. First, though, let's see if I can see anything without getting up."

He paused a little way from the pine, and peered down the hill. Nothing could be seen of the big enclosed field back of the building about which Tom was so careful.

"You have to be up to see anything," mused Ned. "It's up a tree for me! Well, here goes!"

As Ned started to work his way up among the thick, green branches, he became aware, suddenly and somewhat to his surprise, that he was not the only person who knew about the observation spot. For Ned saw, a yard above his head, as he started to climb, two feet, encased in well-made boots, standing on a limb near the trunk of the tree.

"Oh, ho!" mused Ned. "Some one here before me! Where there are feet there must be legs, and where there are legs, most likely a body. And it isn't Harry, either! The feet are too big for that. I wonder—"

But Ned's musings were suddenly cut short, for the person up the tree ahead of him moved quickly and stepped on Ned's fingers, with no light tread.

"Ouch!" exclaimed the young bank clerk involuntarily, and, letting go his hold of the limb, he dropped to the ground, while there came a startled exclamation from the screen of pine branches above him.

Chapter VIII
Detective Rad

"Who's there?" came the demand from the unseen person in the tree.

"I might ask you the same thing," was Ned's sharp retort, as he nursed his skinned and bruised fingers. "What are you doing up there?"

There was no answer, but a sound among the branches indicated that the person up the tree was coming down. In another moment a man leaped to the ground lightly and stood beside Ned. The lad observed that the stranger was clean shaven, except for a small moustache which curled up at the ends slightly.

"For all the world like a small edition of the Kaiser's," Ned described it afterward.

"What are you doing here?" demanded the man, and his voice had in it the ring of authority. It was this very quality that made Ned bristle up and "get on his ear," as he said later. The young clerk did not object to being spoken to authoritatively by those who had the right, but from a stranger it was different.

"I might ask you the same thing," retorted Ned. "I have as much right here as you, I fancy, and I can climb trees, too, but I don't care to have my fingers stepped on," and he looked at the scarified members of his left hand.

"I beg your pardon. I'm sorry if I hurt you. I didn't mean to. And of course this is a public place, in a way, and you have a right here. I was just climbing the tree to—er—to get a fishing pole!"

Ned had all he could do to keep from laughing. The idea of getting a fishing pole from a gnarled and stunted pine struck him as being altogether novel and absurd. Yet it was not time to make fun of the man. The latter looked too serious for that.

"Rather a good view to be had from up where you were, eh?" asked Ned suggestively.

"A good view?" exclaimed the other. "I don't know what you mean!"

"Oh, then you didn't see anything," Ned went on. "Perhaps it's just as well. Are you fond of fishing?"

"Very. I have—But I forget, I do not know you nor you me. Allow me to introduce myself. I am Mr. Walter Simpson, and I am here on a visit I just happened to walk out this way, and, seeing a small stream, thought I should like to fish. I usually carry lines and hooks, and all I needed was the pole. I was looking for it when I heard you, and—"

"I felt you!" interrupted Ned, with a short laugh. He told his own name, but that was all, and seemed about to pass on.

"Are there any locomotive shops around here?" asked Mr. Simpson.

"Locomotive shops?" queried Ned. "None that I know of. Why?"

"Well, I heard heavy machinery being used down there;" and he waved his hand toward Tom's shops, "and I thought—"

"Oh, you mean Shopton!" exclaimed Ned. "That's the Swift plant. No, they don't make locomotives, though they could if they wanted to, for they turn out airships, submarines, tunnel diggers, and I don't know what."

"Do they make munitions there—for the Allies?" asked Mr. Simpson, and there was an eager look on his face.

"No, I don't believe so," Ned answered; "though, in fact, I don't know enough of the place to be in a position to give you any information about it," he told the man, not deeming it wise to go into particulars.

Perhaps the man felt this, as he did not press for an answer.

The two stood looking at one another for some little time, and then the man, with a bow that had in it something of insolence, as well as politeness, turned and went down the path up which Ned had come.

The young bank clerk waited a little while, and then turned his attention to the tree which seemed to have suddenly assumed an importance altogether out of proportion to its size.

"Well, since I'm here I'll have a look up that tree," decided Ned.

Favoring his bruised hand, Ned essayed the ascent of the tree more successfully this time. As he rose up among the branches he found he could look down directly into the yard with the high fence about it. He Could see only a portion, good as his vantage point was, and that portion had in it a few workmen—nothing else.

"No elephants there," said Ned, with a smile, as he remembered Harry's excitement. "Still it's just as well for Tom to know that his place can be looked down on. I'll go and tell him."

As Ned descended the tree he caught a glimpse, off to one side among some bushes, of something moving.

"I wonder if that's my Simp friend, playing I spy?" mused Ned. "Guess I'd better have a look."

He worked his way carefully close to the spot where he had seen the movement. Proceeding then with more caution, watching each step and parting the bushes with a careful hand, Ned beheld what he expected.

There was the late occupant of the pine tree the man who had stepped on Ned's fingers, applying a small telescope to his eye and gazing in the direction of Tom Swift's home.

The man stood concealed in a screen of bushes with his back toward Ned, and seemed oblivious to his surroundings. He moved the glass to and fro, and seemed eagerly intent on discovering something.

"Though what he can see of Tom's place from there isn't much," mused Ned. "I've tried it myself, and I know; you have to be on an elevation to look down. Still it shows he's after something, all right. Guess I'll throw a little scare into him."

As yet, Ned believed himself unobserved, and that his presence was not suspected was proved a moment later when he shouted:

"Hey! What are you doing there?"

He had his eye on the partially concealed man, and the latter, as Ned said afterward, jumped fully two feet in the air, dropping his telescope as he did so, and turning to face the lad.

"Oh, it's you, is it?" he faltered.

"No one else;" and Ned grinned. "Looking for a good place to fish, I presume?"

Then, at least for once, the man's suave manner dropped from him as if it had been a mask. He bared his teeth in a snarl as he answered:

"Mind your own business!"

"Something I'd advise you also to do," replied Ned smoothly. "You can't see anything from there," he went on. "Better go back to the tree and—cut a fishing pole!"

With this parting shot Ned sauntered down the hill, and swung around to make his way toward Tom's home. He paid no further attention to the man, save to determine, by listening, that the fellow was searching among the bushes for the dropped telescope.

The young inventor was at home, taking a hasty lunch which Mrs. Baggert had set out for him, the while he poured over some blueprint drawings that, to Ned's unaccustomed eyes, looked like the mazes of some intricate puzzle.

"Well, where have you been keeping yourself, old man?" asked Tom Swift, after he had greeted his friend.

"I might ask the same of you," retorted Ned, with a smile. "I've been trying to find you to give you some important information, and I made up my mind, after what happened to-day, to write it and leave it for you if I didn't see you."

"What happened to-day?" asked Tom, and there was a serious look on his face.

"You are being spied upon—at least, that part of your works enclosed in the new fence is," replied Ned.

"You don't mean it!" Cried Tom. "This accounts for some of it, then."

"For some of what?" asked Ned.

"For some of the actions of that Blakeson. He's been hanging around here, I understand, asking too many questions about things that I'm trying to keep secret—even from my best friends," and as Tom said this Ned fancied there was a note of regret in his voice.

"Yes, you are keeping some things secret, Tom," said Ned, determined "to take the bull by the horns," as it were.

"I'm sorry, but it has to be," went on Tom. "In a little while—"

"Oh, don't think that I'm at all anxious to know things!" broke in Ned. "I was thinking of some one else, Tom—another of your friends."

"Do you mean Mary?"

Ned nodded.

"She feels rather keenly your lack of explanations," went on the young bank clerk. "If you could only give her a hint—"

"I'm sorry, but it can't be done," and Tom spoke firmly. "But you haven't told me all that happened. You say I am being spied upon."

"Yes," and Ned related what had taken place in the tree.

"Whew!" whistled Tom. "That's going some with a vengeance! I must have that tree down in a jiffy. I didn't imagine there was a spot where the yard could be overlooked. But I evidently skipped that tree. Fortunately it's on land owned by a concern with which I have some connection, and I can have it chopped down without any trouble. Much obliged to you, Ned. I shan't forget this in a hurry. I'll go right away and—"

Tom's further remark was interrupted by the hurried entrance of Eradicate Sampson. The old man was smiling in pleased anticipation, evidently, at the same time, trying hard not to give way to too much emotion.

"I's done it, Massa Tom!" he cried exultingly.

"Done what?" asked the young inventor. "I hope you and Koku haven't had another row."

"No, sah! I don't want nuffin t' do wif dat ornery, low-down white trash! But I's gone an' done whut I said I'd do!"

"What's that, Rad? Come on, tell us! Don't keep us in suspense."

"I's done some deteckertiff wuk, lest laik I said I'd do, an' I's cotched him! By golly, Massa Tom! I's cotched him black-handed, as it says!"

"Caught him? Whom have you caught, Rad?" cried Tom. "Do you suppose he means he's caught the man you saw up the tree, Ned? The man you think is a German spy?"

"It couldn't be. I left him only a little while ago hunting for his telescope."

"Then whom have you caught, Rad?" cried Tom. "Come on, I'll give you credit for it. Tell us!"

"I's cotched dat Dutch Sauerkrauter, dat's who I's cotched, Massa Tom! By golly, I's cotched him!"

"But who, Rad? Who is he?"

"I don't know his name, Massa Tom, but he's a Sauerkrauter, all right. Dat's whut he eats for lunch, an' dat's why I calls him dat. I's cotched him, an' he's locked up in de stable wif mah mule Boomerang. An' ef he tries t' git out Boomerang'll jest natchully kick him into little pieces—dat's whut Boomerang will do, by golly!"

Chapter IX
A Night Test

"Come on, Ned," said Tom, after a moment or two of silent contemplation of Eradicate. "I don't know what this cheerful camouflager of mine is talking about, but we'll have to go to see, I suppose. You say you have shut some one up in Boomerang's stable, Rad?"

"Yes, sah, Massa Tom, dat's whut I's gone an done."

"And you say he's a German?"

"I don't know as to dat, Massa Tom, but he suah done eat sauerkraut 'mostest ebery meal. Dat's whut I call him—a Sauerkrauter! An' he suah was spyin'."

"How do you know that, Rad?"

"'Cause he done went from his own shop on annuder man's ticket into de secret shop, dat's whut he went an' done!"

"Do you mean to tell me, Rad," went on Tom, "that one of the workmen from another shop entered Number Thirteen on the pass issued in the name of one of the men regularly employed in my new shop?"

"Dat's whut he done, Massa Tom."

"How do you know?"

"'Cause I detected him doin' it. Yo'-all done made me a deteckertiff, an' I detected."

"Go on, Rad."

"Well, sah, Massa Tom, I seen dish yeah Dutchman git a ticket-pass offen one ob de reg'lar men. Den he went in de unlucky place an' stayed fo' a long time. When he come out I jest natchully nabbed him, dat's whut I done, an' I took him to Boomerang's stable."

"How'd you get him to go with you?" asked Ned, for the old colored man was feeble, and most of the men employed at Tom's plant were of a robust type.

"I done fooled him. I said as how I'd jest brought from town in mah mule cart some new sauerkraut, an' he could sample it if he liked. So he went wif me, an' when I got him to de stable I pushed him in and locked de door!"

"Come on!" cried Tom to his chum. "Rad may be right, after all, and one of my workmen may be a German spy, though I've tried to weed them all out.

"However, no matter about that, if he was employed in another shop, he had no right to go into Number Thirteen. That's a violation of rules. But if he's in Rad's ramshackle stable he can easily get out."

"No, sah, dat's whut he can't do!" insisted the colored man.

"Why not?" asked Tom.

"'Cause Boomerang's on guard, an' yo'-all knows how dat mule of mine can use his heels!"

"I know, Rad," went on Tom; "but this fellow will find a way of keeping out of their way. We must hurry."

"Oh, he's safe enough," declared the colored man. "I done tole Koku to stan' guard, too! Dat low-down white trash ob a giant is all right fo' guardin', but he ain't wuff shucks at detectin'!" said Eradicate, with pardonable pride. "By golly, maybe I's too old t' put on guard, but I kin detect, all right!"

"If this proves true, I'll begin to believe you can," replied Tom. "Hop along, Ned!"

Followed by the shuffling and chuckling negro, Tom and Ned went to the rather insecure stable where the mule Boomerang was kept. That is, the stable was insecure from the standpoint of a jail. But the sight of the giant Koku marching up and down in front of the place, armed with a big club, reassured Tom.

"Is he in there, Koku?" asked the young inventor.

"Yes, Master! He try once come out, but he approach his head very close my defense weapon and he go back again."

"I should think he would," laughed Ned, as he noted the giant's club.

"Well, Rad, let's have a look at your prisoner. Open the door, Koku," commanded Tom.

"Better look out," advised Ned. "He may be armed."

"We'll have to take a chance. Besides, I don't believe he is, or he'd have fired at Koku. There isn't much to fear with the giant ready for emergencies. Now we'll see who he is. I can't imagine one of my men turning traitor."

The door was opened and a rather miserable-looking man shuffled out. There was a bloody rag on his head, and he seemed to have made more of an effort to escape than Koku described, for he appeared to have suffered in the ensuing fight.

"Carl Schwen!" exclaimed Tom. "So it was you, was it?"

The German, for such he was, did not answer for a moment. He appeared downcast, and as if suffering. Then a change came over him. He straightened up, saluted as a soldier might have done, and a sneering look came into his face. It was succeeded by one of pride as the man exclaimed:

"Yes, it is I! And I tried to do what I tried to do for the Fatherland! I have failed. Now you will have me shot as a spy, I suppose!" he added bitterly.

Tom did not answer directly. He looked keenly at the man, and at last said:

"I am sorry to see this. I knew you were a German, Schwen, but I kept you employed at work that could not, by any possibility, be considered as used against your country. You are a good machinist, and I needed you. But if what I hear about you is true, it is the end."

"It is the end," said the man simply. "I tried and failed. If it had not been for Eradicate—Well, he's smarter than I gave him credit for, that's all!"

The man spoke very good English, with hardly a trace of German accent, but there was no doubt as to his character.

"What will you do with him, Tom?" asked Ned.

"I don't know. I'll have to do a little investigating first. But he must be locked up. Schwen," went on the young inventor, "I'm sorry about this, but I shall have to give you into the custody of a United States marshal. You are not a naturalized citizen, are you?"

The man muttered something in German to the effect that he was not naturalized and was glad of it.

"Then you come under the head of an enemy alien," decided Tom, who understood what was said, "and will have to be interned. I had hoped to avoid this, but it seems it cannot be. I am sorry to lose you, but there are more important matters. Now let's get at the bottom of this."

Schwen was, after a little delay, taken in charge by the proper officer, and then a search was made of his room, for, in common with some of the other workmen, he lived in a boarding house not far from the plant.

There, by a perusal of his papers, enough was revealed to show Tom the danger he had escaped.

"And yet I don't know that I have altogether escaped it," he said to Ned, as they talked it over. "There's no telling how long this spy work may have been going on. If he has discovered all the secrets of Shop Thirteen it may be a bad thing for the Allies and—"

"Look out!" warned Ned, with a laugh. "You'll be saying things you don't want to, Tom and not at all in keeping with your former silence."

"That's so," agreed the young inventor, with a sigh. "But if things go right I'll not have to keep silent much longer. I may be able to tell you everything."

"Don't tell me—tell Mary," advised his chum. "She feels your silence more than I do. I know how such things are."

"Well, I'll be able to tell her, too," decided Tom. "That is, if Schwen hasn't spoiled everything. Look here, Ned, these papers show he's been in correspondence with Blakeson and Grinder."

"What about, Tom?"

"I can't tell. The letters are evidently written in code, and I can't translate it offhand. But I'll make another attempt at it. And here's one from a person who signs himself Walter Simpson, but the writing is in German."

"Walter Simpson!" cried Ned. "That's my friend of the tree!"

"It is?" cried Tom. "Then things begin to fit themselves together. Simpson is a spy, and he was probably trying to communicate with Schwen. But the latter didn't get the information he wanted, or, if he did get it, he wasn't able to pass it on to the man in the tree. Eradicate nipped him just in time."

And, so it seemed, the colored man had done. By accident he had discovered that Schwen had prevailed on one of the workmen in Shop 13 to change passes with him. This enabled the German spy to gain admittance to the secret place, which Tom thought was so well guarded. The man who let Schwen take the pass was in the game, too, it appeared, and he was also placed under arrest. But he was a mere tool in the pay of the others, and had no chance to gain valuable information.

A hasty search of Shop 13 did not reveal anything missing, and it was surmised (for Schwen would not talk) that he had not found time to go about and get all that he was after.

Soon after Schwen's arrest the "Spy Tree," as Tom called it, was cut down.

"Eradicate certainly did better than I ever expected he would," declared Tom. "Well, if all goes well, there won't be so much need for secrecy after a day or so. We're going to give her a test, and then—"

"Give who a test?" asked Ned, with a smile.

"You'll soon see," answered Tom, with an answering grin. "I hereby invite you and Mr. Damon to come over to Shop Thirteen day after to-morrow night and then—Well, you'll see what you'll see."

With this Ned had to be content, and he waited anxiously for the appointed time to come.

"I surely will be glad when Tom is more like himself," he mused, as he left his chum. "And I guess Mary will be, too. I wonder if he's going to ask her to the exhibition?"

It developed that Tom had done so, a fact which Ned learned on the morning of the day set for the test.

"Come over about nine o'clock," Tom said to his chum. "I guess it will be dark enough then."

Meanwhile Schwen and Otto Kuhn, the other man involved, had been locked up, and all their papers given into the charge of the United States authorities. A closer guard than ever was kept over No. 13 shop, and some of the workmen, against whom there was a slight suspicion, were transferred.

"Well, we'll see what we shall see," mused Ned on the appointed evening, when a telephone message from Mr. Damon informed the young bank clerk that the eccentric man was coming to call for him before going on to the Swift place.

Chapter X
A Runaway Giant

"What do you think it's all about, Mr. Damon?"

"I'm sure I don't know, Ned."

The two were at the home of the young bank clerk, preparing to start for the Swift place, it being nearly nine o'clock on the evening named by the youthful inventor.

"Bless my hat-rack!" went on the eccentric man, "but Tom isn't at all like himself of late. He's working on some invention, I know that, but it's all I do know. He hasn't given me a hint of it."

"Nor me, nor any of his friends," added Ned. "And he acts so oddly about enlisting—doesn't want even to speak of it. How he got exempted I don't know, but I do know one thing, and that is Tom Swift is for Uncle Sam first, last and always!"

"Oh, of course!" agreed Mr. Damon. "Well, we'll soon know, I guess. We'd better start, Ned."

"It's useless to try to guess what it is Tom is up to. He has kept his secret well. The nearest any one has come to it was when Harry figured out that Tom had a band of giant elephants which he was fitting with coats of steel armor to go against the Germans," observed Ned, when he and Mr. Damon were on their way.

"Well, that mightn't be so bad," agreed Mr. Damon. "But—um—elephants—and wild giant ones, too! Bless my circus ticket, Ned! do you think we'd better go in that case?"

"Oh, Tom hasn't anything like that!" laughed Ned. "That was only Harry's crazy notion after he saw something big and ungainly careening about the enclosed yard of Shop Thirteen. Hello, there go Mary Nestor and her father!" and Ned pointed to the opposite side of the street where the girl and Mr. Nestor could be seen in the light of a street lamp.

"They're going out to see Tom's secret," said Mr. Damon. "There's plenty of room in my car. Let's ask them to go with us."

"Surely," agreed Ned, and a moment later he and Mary were in the rear seat while Mr. Damon and Mr. Nestor were in the front, Mr. Damon at the wheel, and they were soon speeding down the road.

"I do hope everything will go all right," observed Mary.

"What do you mean?" asked Ned.

"I mean Tom is a little bit anxious about this test."

"Did he tell you what it was to be?"

"No; but when he called to invite father and me to be present he seemed worried. I guess it's a big thing, for he never has acted this way before—not talking about his work."

"That's right," assented Ned. "But the secret will soon be disclosed, I fancy. But how is it you aren't going to the dance with Lieutenant Martin? He told me you had half accepted for to-night."

"I had." And if it had been light enough Ned would have seen Mary blushing. "I was going with him. It's a dance for the benefit of the Red Cross to get money for comfort kits for the soldiers. But when Tom sent word that he'd like to have me present to-night, why—"

"Oh, I see!" broke in Ned, with a little laugh. "'Nough said!"

Mary's blushes were deeper, but the kindly night hid them.

Then they conversed on matters connected with the big war—the selling of Liberty Bonds, the Red Cross work and the Surgical Dressings Committee, in which Mary was the head of a junior league.

"Everybody in Shopton seems to be doing something to help win the war," said Mary, and as there was just then a lull in the talk between her father and Mr. Damon her words sounded clearly.

"Yes, everybody—that is, all but a few," said Mr. Nestor, "and they ought to get busy. There are some young fellows in this town that ought to be wearing khaki, and I don't mean you, Ned Newton. You're doing your bit, all right."

"And so is Tom Swift!" exclaimed Mr. Damon, as if there had been an implied accusation against the young inventor. "I heard, only to-day, that one of his inventions—a gas helmet that he planned—is in use on the Western front in Europe. Tom gave his patents to the government, and even made a lot of the helmets free to show other factories how to turn them out to advantage."

"He did?" cried Mr. Nestor.

"That's what he did. Talk about doing your bit—"

"I didn't know that," observed Mary's father slowly. "Do you suppose it's a test of another gas helmet that Tom has asked us out to see to-night?"

"I hardly think so," said Ned. "He wouldn't wait until after dark for that. This is something big, and Tom must intend to have it out in the open. He probably waited until after sunset so the neighbors wouldn't come out in flocks. There's been a lot of talk about what is going on in Shop Thirteen, especially since the arrest of the German spies, and the least hint that a test is under way would bring out a big crowd."

"I suppose so," agreed Mr. Nestor. "Well, I'm glad to know that Tom is doing something for Uncle Sam, even if it's only helping with gas helmets. Those Germans are barbarians, if ever there were any, and we've got to fight them the same way they fight us! That's the only way to end the war! Now if I had my way, I'd take every German I could lay my hands on—"

"Father, pretzels!" exclaimed Mary.

"Eh? What's that, my dear?"

"I said pretzels!"

"Oh!" and Mr. Nestor's voice lost its sharpness.

"That's my way of quieting father down when he gets too strenuous in his talk about the war," explained Mary. "We agreed that whenever he got excited I was to say 'pretzels' to him, and that would make him remember. We made up our little scheme after he got into an argument with a man on the train and was carried past his station."

"That's right," admitted Mr. Nestor, with a laugh. "But that fellow was the most obstinate, pig-headed Dutchman that ever tackled a plate of pig's knuckles and sauerkraut, and if he had the least grain of common sense he'd—"

"Pretzels!" cried Mary.

"Eh? Oh, yes, my dear. I was forgetting again."

There was a moment of merriment, and then, after the talk had run for a while in other and safer channels, Mr. Damon made the announcement:

"I think we're about there. We'll be at Tom's place when we make the turn and—"

He was interrupted by a low, heavy rumbling.

"What's that?" asked Mr. Nestor.

"It's getting louder—the noise," remarked Mary. "It sounds as if some big body were approaching down the road—the tramp of many feet. Can it be that troops are marching away?"

"Bless my spark plug!" suddenly cried Mr. Damon. "Look!"

They gazed ahead, and there, seen in the glare of the automobile headlights, was an immense, dark body approaching them from across a level field. The rumble and roar became more pronounced and the ground shook as though from an earthquake.

A glaring light shone out from the ponderous moving body, and above the roar and rattle a voice called:

"Out out of the way! We've lost control! Look out!"

"Bless my steering wheel!" gasped Mr. Damon, "that was Tom Swift's voice! But what is he doing in that—thing?"

"It must be his new invention!" exclaimed Ned.

"What is it?" asked Mr. Nestor.

"A giant," ventured Ned. "It's a giant machine of some sort and—"

"And it's running away!" cried Mr. Damon, as he quickly steered his car to one side—and not a moment too soon! An instant later in a cloud of dust, and with a rumble and a roar as of a dozen express trains fused into one, the runaway giant—of what nature they could only guess—flashed and lumbered by, Tom Swift leaning from an opening in the thick steel side, and shouting something to his friends.

Chapter XI
Tom's Tank

"What was it?" gasped Mary, and, to her surprise, she found herself close to Ned, clutching his arm.

"I have an idea, but I'd rather let Tom tell you," he answered.

"But where's it going?" asked Mr. Nestor. "What in the world does Tom Swift mean by inviting us out here to witness a test, and then nearly running us down under a Juggernaut?"

"Oh, there must be some mistake, I'm sure," returned his daughter. "Tom didn't intend this."

"But, bless my insurance policy, look at that thing go! What in the world is it?" cried Mr. Damon.

The "thing" was certainly going. It had careened from the road, tilted itself down into a ditch and gone on across the fields, lights shooting from it in eccentric fashion.

"Maybe we'd better take after it," suggested Mr. Nestor. "If Tom is—"

"There, it's stopping!" cried Ned. "Come on!"

He sprang from the automobile, helped Mary to get out, and then the two, followed by Mr. Damon and Mr. Nestor, made their way across the fields toward the big object where it had come to a stop, the rumbling and roaring ceasing.

Before the little party reached the strange machine—the "runaway giant," as they dubbed it in their excitement—a bright light flashed from it, a light that illuminated their path right up to the monster. And in the glare of this light they saw Tom Swift stepping out through a steel door in the side of the affair.

"Are you all right?" he called to his friends, as they approached.

"All right, as nearly as we can be when we've been almost scared to death, Tom," said Mr. Nestor.

"I'm surely sorry for what happened," Tom answered, with a relieved laugh. "Part of the steering gear broke and I had to guide it by operating the two motors alternately. It can be worked that way, but it takes a little practice to become expert."

"I should say so!" cried Mr. Damon. "But what in the world does it all mean, Tom Swift? You invite us out to see something—"

"And there she is!" interrupted the young inventor. "You saw her a little before I meant you to, and not under exactly the circumstances I had planned. But there she is!" And he turned as though introducing the metallic monster to his friends.

"What is she, Tom?" asked Ned. "Name it!"

"My latest invention, or rather the invention of my father and myself," answered Tom, and his voice showed the love and reverence he felt for his parent. "Perhaps I should say adaptation instead of invention," Tom went on, "since that is what it is. But, at any rate, it's my latest—dad's and mine—and it's the newest, biggest, most improved and powerful fighting tank that's been turned out of any shop, as far as I can learn.

"Ladies—I mean lady and gentlemen—allow me to present to you War Tank A, and may she rumble till the pride of the Boche is brought low and humble!" cried Tom.

"Hurray! That's what I say!" cheered Ned.

"That's what I have been at work on lately. I'll give you a little history of it, and then you may come inside and have a ride home."

"In that?" cried Mr. Damon.

"Yes. I can't promise to move as speedily as your car, but I can make better time than the British tanks. They go about six miles an hour, I understand, and I've got mine geared to ten. That's one improvement dad and I have made."

"Ride in that!" cried Mr. Nestor. "Tom, I like you, and I'm glad to see I've been mistaken about you. You have been doing your bit, after all; but—"

"Oh, I've only begun!" laughed Tom Swift.

"Well, no matter about that. However much I like you," went on Mr. Nestor, "I'd as soon ride on the wings of a thunderbolt as in Tank A, Tom Swift."

"Oh, it isn't as bad as that!" laughed the young scientist. "But neither is it a limousine. However, come inside, anyhow, and I'll tell you something about it. Then I guess we can guide it back. The men are repairing the break."

The visitors entered the great craft through the door by which Tom had emerged. At first all they saw was a small compartment, with walls of heavy steel, some shelves of the same and a seat which folded up against the wall made of like powerful material.

"This is supposed to be the captain's room, where he stays when he directs matters." Tom explained. "The machinery is below and beyond here."

"How'd you come to evolve this?" asked Ned. "I haven't seen half enough of the outside, to say nothing of the inside."

"You'll have time enough," Tom said. "This is my first completed tank. There are some improvements to be made before we send it to the other side to be copied.

"Then they'll make them in England as well as here, and from here we'll ship them in sections."

"I don't see how you ever thought of it!" exclaimed the girl, in wonder.

"Well, I didn't all at once," Tom answered, with a laugh. "It came by degrees. I first got the idea when I heard of the British tanks.

"When I had read how they went into action and what they accomplished against the barbed wire entanglements, and how they crossed the trenches, I concluded that a bigger tank, one capable of more speed, say ten or twelve miles an hour, and one that could cross bigger excavations—the English tanks up to this time can cross a ditch of twelve feet—I thought that, with one made on such specifications, more effective work could be done against the Germans."

"And will yours do that?" asked Ned. "I mean will it do ten miles an hour, and straddle over a wider ditch than twelve feet?"

"It'll do both," promptly answered Tom. "We did a little better than eleven miles an hour a while ago when I yelled to you to get out of the way just now. It's true we weren't under good control, but the speed had nothing to do with that. And as for going over a big ditch, I think we straddled one about fourteen feet across back there, and we can do better when I get my grippers to working."

"Grippers!" exclaimed Mary.

"What kind of trench slang is that, Tom Swift?" asked Mr. Damon.

"Well, that's a new idea I'm going to try out It's something like this," and while from a distant part of the interior of Tank A came the sound of hammering, the young inventor rapidly drew a rough pencil sketch.

It showed the tank in outline, much as appear the pictures of tanks already in service—the former simile of two wedge-shaped pieces of metal put together broad end to broad end, still holding good. From one end of the tank, as Tom drew it, there extended two long arms of latticed steel construction.

"The idea is," said Tom, "to lay these down in front of the tank, by means of cams and levers operated from inside. If we get to a ditch which we can't climb down into and out again, or bridge with the belt caterpillar wheels, we'll use the grippers. They'll be laid down, taking a grip on the far side of the trench, and we'll slide across on them."

"And leave them there?" asked Mr. Damon.

"No, we won't leave them. We'll pick them up after we have passed over them and use them in front again as we need them. A couple of extra pairs of grippers may be carried for emergencies, but I plan to use the same ones over and over again."

"But what makes it go?" asked Mary. "I don't want all the details, Tom," she said, with a smile, "but I'd like to know what makes your tank move."

"I'll be able to show you in a little while," he answered. "But it may be enough now if I tell you that the main power consists of two big gasolene engines, one on either side. They can be geared to operate together or separately. And these engines turn the endless belts made of broad, steel plates, on which the tank travels. The belts pass along the outer edges of the tank longitudinally, and go around cogged wheels at either end of the blunt noses.

"When both belts travel at the same rate of speed the tank goes in a straight line, though it can be steered from side to side by means of a trailer wheel in the rear. Making one belt—one set of caterpillar wheels, you know—go faster than the other will make the tank travel to one side or the other, the turn being in the direction of the slowest moving belt. In this way we can steer when the trailer wheels are broken."

"And what does your tank do except travel along, not minding a hail of bullets?" asked Mr. Nestor.

"Well," answered Tom, "it can do anything any other tank can do, and then some more. It can demolish a good-sized house or heavy wall, break down big trees, and chew up barbed-wire fences as if they were toothpicks. I'll show you all that in due time. Just now, if the repairs are finished, we can get back on the road—"

At that moment a door leading into the compartment where Tom and his friends were talking opened, and one of the workmen said:

"A man outside asking to see you, Mr. Swift."

"Pardon me, but I won't keep you a moment," interrupted a suave voice. "I happened to observe your tank, and I took the liberty of entering to see—"

"Simpson!" cried Ned Newton, as he recognized the man who had been up the tree. "It's that spy, Simpson, Tom!"

Chapter XII
Bridging a Gap

Such surprise showed both on the face of Ned Newton and that of the man who called himself Walter Simpson that it would be hard to say which was in the greater degree. For a moment the newcomer stood as if he had received all electric shock, and was incapable of motion. Then, as the echoes of Ned's voice died away and the young bank clerk, being the first to recover from the shock, made a motion toward the unwelcome and uninvited intruder, Simpson exclaimed.

"I will not bother now. Some other time will do as well."

Then, with a haste that could be called nothing less than precipitate, he made a turn and fairly shot out of the door by which he had entered the tank.

"There he goes!" cried Mr. Damon. "Bless my speedometer, but there he goes!"

"I'll stop him!" cried Ned. "We've got to find out more about him! I'll get him, Tom!"

Tom Swift was not one to let a friend rush alone into what might be danger. He realized immediately what his chum meant when he called out the identity of the intruder, and, wishing to clear up some of the mystery of which he became aware when Schwen was arrested and the paper showing a correspondence with this Simpson were found, Tom darted out to try to assist in the capture.

"He went this way!" cried Ned, who was visible in the glare of the searchlight that still played its powerful beams over the stern of the tank, if such an ungainly machine can be said to have a bow and stern. "Over this way!"

"I'm with you!" cried Tom. "See if you can pick up that man who just ran out of here!" he cried to the operator of the searchlight in the elevated observation section of what corresponded to the conning tower of a submarine.

This was a sort of lookout box on top of the tank, containing, among other machines, the searchlight. "Pick him up!" cried Tom.

The operator flashed the intense white beam, like a finger of light, around in eccentric circles, but though this brought into vivid relief the configuration of the field and road near which the tank was stalled, it showed no running fugitive. Tom and Ned were observed—shadows of black in the glare—by Mary and her friends in the tank, but there was no one else.

"Come on!" cried Ned. "We can find him, Tom!"

But this was easier said than done. Even though they were aided by the bright light, they caught no glimpse of the man who called himself Simpson.

"Guess he got away," said Tom, when he and Ned had circled about and investigated many clumps of bushes, trees, stumps and other barriers that might conceal the fugitive.

"I guess so," agreed Ned. "Unless he's hiding in what we might call a shell crater."

"Hardly that," and Tom smiled. "Though if all goes well the men who operate this tank later may be searching for men in real shell holes."

"Is this one going to the other side?" asked Ned, as the two walked back toward the tank.

"I hope it will be the first of my new machines on the Western front," Tom answered. "But I've still got to perfect it in some details and then take it apart. After that, if it comes up to expectations, we'll begin making them in quantities."

"Did you get him?" asked Mr. Damon eagerly, as the two young men came back to join Mary and her friends.

"No, he got away," Tom answered.

"Did he try to blow up the tank?" asked Mr. Nestor, who had an abnormal fear of explosives. "Was he a German spy?"

"I think he's that, all right," said Ned grimly. "As to his endeavoring to blow up Tom's tank, I believe him capable of it, though he didn't try it to-night—unless he's planted a time bomb somewhere about, Tom."

"Hardly, I guess," answered the young inventor. "He didn't have a chance to do that. Anyhow we won't remain here long. Now, Ned, what about this chap? Is he really the one you saw up in the tree?"

"I not only saw him but I felt him," answered Ned, with a rueful look at his fingers. "He stepped right on me. And when he came inside the tank to-night I knew him at once. I guess he was as surprised to see me as I was to see him."

"But what was his object?" asked Mr. Nestor.

"He must have some connection with my old enemy, Blakeson," answered Tom, "and we know he's mixed up with Schwen. From the looks of him I should say that this Simpson, as he calls himself, is the directing head of the whole business. He looks to be the moneyed man, and the brains of the plotters. Blakeson is smart, in a mechanical way, and Schwen is one of the best machinists I've ever employed. But this Simpson strikes me as being the slick one of the trio."

"But what made him come here, and what did he want?" asked Mary. "Dear me! it's like one of those moving picture plots, only I never saw one with a tank in it before—I mean a tank like yours, Tom."

"Yes, it is a bit like moving picture—especially chasing Simpson by searchlight," agreed the young inventor. "As to what he wanted, I suppose he came to spy out some of my secret inventions—dad's and mine. He's probably been hiding and sneaking around the works ever since we arrested Schwen. Some of my men have reported seeing strangers about, but I have kept Shop Thirteen well guarded.

"However, this fellow may have been waiting outside, and he may have followed the tank when we started off a little while ago for the night test. Then, when he saw our mishap and noticed that we were stalled, he came in, boldly enough, thinking, I suppose, that, as I had never seen him, he would take a chance on getting as much information as he could in a hurry."

"But he didn't count on Ned's being here!" chuckled Mr. Damon.

"No; that's where he slipped a cog," remarked Mr. Nestor. "Well, Tom, I like your tank, what I've seen of her, but it's getting late and I think Mary and I had better be getting back home."

"We'll be ready to start in a little while," Tom said, after a brief consultation with one of his men. "Still, perhaps it would be just as well if you didn't ride back with me. She may go all right, and then, again, she may not. And as it's dark, and we're in a rough part of the field, you might be a bit shaken up. Not that the tank minds it!" the young inventor hastened to add "She's got to do her bit over worse places than this—much worse—but I want to get her in a little better working shape first. So if you don't mind, Mary, I'll postpone your initial trip."

"Oh, I don't mind, Tom! I'm so glad you've made this! I want to see the war ended, and I think machines like this will help."

"I'll ride back with you, Tom, if you don't mind," put in Ned. "I guess a little shaking up won't hurt me."

"All right—stick. We're going to start very soon."

"Well, I'm coming over to-morrow to have a look at it by daylight," said Mr. Damon, as he started toward his car.

"So am I," added Mary. "Please call for me, Mr. Damon."

"I will," he promised.

Mr. Nestor, his daughter, and Mr. Damon went back to the automobile, while Ned remained with Tom. In a little while those in the car heard once more the rumbling and roaring sound and felt the earth tremble. Then, with a flashing of lights, the big, ungainly shape of the tank lifted herself out of the little ditch in which she had come to a halt, and began to climb back to the road.

Ned Newton stood beside Tom in the control tower of the great tank as she started on her homeward way.

"Isn't it wonderful!" murmured Mary, as she saw Tank A lumbering along toward the road. "Oh, and to think that human beings made that. To think that Tom should know how to build such a wonderful machine!"

"And run it, too, Mary! That's the point! Make it run!" cried her father. "I tell you, that Tom Swift is a wonder!"

"Bless my dictionary, he sure is!" agreed Mr. Damon.

Along the road, back toward the shop whence it had emerged, rumbled the tank. The noise brought to their doors inhabitants along the country thoroughfare, and some of them were frightened when they saw Tom Swift's latest war machine, the details of which they could only guess at in the darkness.

"She'll butt over a house if it gets in her path, knock down trees, chew up barbed-wire, and climb down into ravines and out again, and go over a good-sized stream without a whimper," said Tom, as he steered the great machine.

There was little chance then for Ned to see much of the inside mechanism of the tank. He observed that Tom, standing in the forward tower, steered it very easily by a small wheel or by a lever, alternately, and that he communicated with the engine room by means of electric signals.

"And she steers by electricity, too," Tom told his friend. "That was one difficulty with the first tanks. They had to be steered by brute force, so to speak, and it was a terrific strain on the man in the tower. Now I can guide this in two ways: by the electric mechanism which swings the trailer wheels to either side, or by varying the speed of the two motors that work the caterpillar belts. So if one breaks down, I have the other."

"Got any guns aboard her—I mean machine guns?" asked Ned.

"Not yet. But I'm going to install some. I wanted to get the tank in proper working order first. The guns are only incidental, though of course they're vitally necessary when she goes into action. I've got 'em all ready to put in. But first I'm going to try the grippers."

"Oh, you mean the gap-bridgers?" asked Ned.

"That's it," answered Tom. "Look out, we're going over a rough spot now."

And they did. Ned was greatly shaken up, and fairly tossed from side to side of the steering tower. For the tank contained no springs, except such as were installed around the most delicate machinery, and it was like riding in a dump cart over a very rough road.

"However, that's part of the game," Tom observed.

Tank A reached her "harbor" safely—in other words, the machine shop enclosed by the high fence, inside of which she had been built.

Tom and Ned made some inquiries of Koku and Eradicate as to whether or not there had been any unusual sights or sounds about the place. They feared Simpson might have come to the shop to try to get possession of important drawings or data.

But all had been quiet, Koku reported. Nor had Eradicate seen or heard anything out of the ordinary.

"Then I guess we'll lock up and turn in," decided Tom. "Come over to-morrow, Ned."

"I will," promised the young bank clerk. "I want to see more of what makes the wheels go round." And he laughed at his own ingenuousness.

The next day Tom showed his friends as much as they cared to see about the workings of the tank. They inspected the powerful gasolene engines, saw how they worked the endless belts made of plates of jointed steel, which, running over sprocket wheels, really gave the tank its power by providing great tractive force.

Any self-propelled vehicle depends for its power, either to move itself or to push or to pull, on its tractive force—that is, the grip it can get on the ground.

In the case of a bicycle little tractive power is needed, and this is provided by the rubber tires, which grip the ground. A locomotive depends for its tractive power on its weight pressing on its driving wheels, and the more driving wheels there are and the heavier the locomotive, the more it can pull, though in that case speed is lost. This is why freight locomotives are so heavy and have so many large driving wheels. They pull the engine along, and the cars also, by their weight pressing on the rails.

The endless steel belts of a tank are, the same as the wheels of a locomotive. And the belts, being very broad, which gives them a large surface with which to press on the ground, and the tank being very heavy, great power to advance is thus obtained, though at the sacrifice of speed. However, Tom Swift had made his tank so that it would do about ten miles and more an hour, nearly double the progress obtained up to that time by the British machines.

His visitors saw the great motors, they inspected the compact but not very attractive living quarters of the crew, for provision had to be made for the men to stay in the tank if, perchance, it became stalled in No Man's Land, surrounded by the enemy.

The tank was powerfully armored and would be armed. There were a number of machine guns to be installed, quick-firers of various types, and in addition the tank could carry a number of riflemen.

It was upon the crushing power of the tank, though, that most reliance was placed. Thus it could lead the way for an infantry advance through the enemy's lines, making nothing of barbed wire that would take an artillery fire of several days to cut to pieces.

"And now, Ned," said Tom, about a week after the night test of the tank, "I'm going to try what she'll do in bridging a gap."

"Have you got her in shape again?"

"Yes, everything is all right. I've taken out the weak part in the steering gear that nearly caused us to run you down, and we're safe in that respect now. And I've got the grippers made. It only remains to see whether they're strong enough to bear the weight of my little baby," and Tom affectionately patted the steel sides of Tank A.

While his men were getting the machine ready for a test out on the road, and for a journey across a small stream not far away, Tom told his chum about conceiving the idea for the tank and carrying it out secretly with the aid of his father and certain workmen.

"That's the reason the government exempted me from enlisting," Tom said. "They wanted me to finish this tank. I didn't exactly want to, but I considered it my 'bit.' After this I'm going into the army, Ned."

"Glad to hear it, old man. Maybe by that time I'll have this Liberty Bond work finished, and I'll go with you. We'll have great times together! Have you heard anything more of Simpson, Blakeson and Scoundrels?" And Ned laughed as he named this "firm."

"No," answered Tom. "I guess we scared off that slick German spy."

Once more the tank lumbered out along the road. It was a mighty engine of war, and inside her rode Tom and Ned. Mary and her father had been invited, but the girl could not quite get her courage to the point of accepting, nor did Mr. Nestor care to go. Mr. Damon, however, as might be guessed, was there.

"Bless my monkey wrench, Tom!" cried the eccentric man, as he noted their advance over some rough ground, "are you really going to make this machine cross Tinkle Creek on a bridge of steel you carry with you?"

"I'm going to try, Mr. Damon."

A little later, after a successful test up and down a small gully, Tank A arrived at the edge of Tinkle Creek, a small stream about twenty feet wide, not far from Tom's home. At the point selected for the test the banks were high and steep.

"If she bridges that gap she'll do anything," murmured Ned, as the tank came to a stop on the edge.

Chapter XIII
Into a Trench

Tom cast a hasty glance over the mechanism of the machine before he started to cross the stream by the additional aid of the grippers, or spanners, as he sometimes called this latest device.

Along each side, in a row of sockets, were two long girders of steel, latticed like the main supports of a bridge. They were of peculiar triangular construction, designed to support heavy weights, and each end was broadly flanged to prevent its sinking too deeply into the earth on either side of a gully or a stream.

The grippers also had a sort of clawlike arrangement on either end, working on the principle of an "orange-peel" shovel, and these claws were designed to grip the earth to prevent slipping.

The spanners would be pulled out from their sockets on the side of the tank by means of steel cables, which were operated from within. They would be run out across the gap and fastened in place. The tank was designed to travel along them to the other side of the gap, and, once there, to pick up the girders, slip them back into place on the sides, and the engine of war would travel on.

"You are mightily excited, Tom.

"I admit it, Ned. You see, I have not tried the grippers out except on a small model. They worked there, but whether they will work in practice remains to be seen. Of course, at this stage, I'm willing to stake my all on the results, but there is always a half-question until the final try-out under practical conditions."

"Well, we'll soon see," said one of the workmen. "Are you ready, Mr. Swift?"

"All ready," answered Tom.

Tank A, as she was officially known, had come to a stop, as has been said, on the very edge of Tinkle Creek. The banks were fairly solid here, and descended precipitously to the water ten feet below. The shores were about twenty feet apart.

"Suppose the spanners break when you're halfway over, Tom?" asked his chum.

"I don't like to suppose anything of the sort. But if they do, we're going down!"

"Can you get up again?"

"That remains to be seen," was the non-committal reply. "Well, here goes, anyhow!"

Going up into the observation tower, which was only slightly raised above the roof of the highest part of the tank, Tom gave the signal for the motors to start. There was a trembling throughout the whole of the vast structure. Tom threw back a lever and Ned, peering from a side observation slot, beheld a strange sight.

Like the main arm of some great steam shovel, two long, latticed girders of steel shot out from the sides of the tank. They gave a half turn, as they were pulled forward by the steel ropes, so that they lay with their broader surfaces uppermost.

Straight across the stream they were pulled, their clawlike ends coming to a rest on the opposite bank. Then they were tightened into place by a backward pull on the operating cables, and Tom, with a sigh of relief, announced:

"Well, so far so good!"

"Do we go over now?" inquired Ned.

"Over the top—yes, I hope," answered Tom, with a laugh. "How about you down there?" he called to the engine room through a telephone which could only be used when the machinery was not in action, there being too much noise to permit the use of any but visual signals after that.

"All right," came back the answer. "We're ready when you are."

"Then here we go!" said Tom. "Hold fast, Ned! Of course there's no real telling what will happen, though I believe we'll come out of it alive."

"Cheerful prospect," murmured Ned.

The grippers were now in place. It only remained for the tank to propel herself over them, pick them up on the other side of Tinkle Creek, and proceed on her course.

Tom Swift hesitated a moment, one hand on the starting lever and the other on the steering wheel. Then, with a glance at Ned, half whimsical and half resolute, Tom started Tank A on what might prove to be her last journey.

Slowly the ponderous caterpillar belts moved around on the sprocket wheels. They ground with a clash of steel on the surface of the spanners. So long was the tank that the forward end, or the "nose," was halfway across the stream before the bottom part of the endless belts gripped the latticed bridge.

"If we fall, we'll span the creek, not fall into it," murmured Ned, as he looked from the observation slot.

"That's what I counted on," Tom said. "We'll get out, even if we do fall."

But Tank A was not destined to fall. In another moment her entire weight rested on the novel and transportable bridge Tom Swift had evolved. Then, as the gripping ends of the girders sank farther into the soil, the tank went on her way.

Slowly, at half speed, she crawled over the steel beams, making progress over the creek and as safely above the water as though on a regularly constructed bridge.

On and on she went. Now her entire weight was over the middle of the temporary structures. If they were going to give way at all, it would be at this point. But they did not give. The latticed and triangular steel, than which there is no stronger form of construction, held up the immense weight of Tank A, and on this novel bridge she propelled herself across Tinkle Creek.

"Well, the worst is over," remarked Ned, as he saw the nose of the tank project beyond the farthermost bank.

"Yes, even if they collapse now nothing much can happen," Tom answered. "It won't be any worse than wallowing down into a trench and out again. But I think the spanners will hold."

And hold they did! They held, giving way not a fraction of an inch, until the tank was safely across, and then, after a little delay, due to a jamming of one of the recovery cables, the spanners were picked up, slid into the receiving sockets, and the great war engine was ready to proceed again.

"Hurrah!" cried Ned. "She did it, Tom, old man!" and he clapped his chum resoundingly on the back.

"She certainly did!" was the answer. "But you needn't knock me apart telling me that. Go easy!"

"Bless my apple pie!" cried Mr. Damon, who was as much pleased as either of the boys, "this is what I call great!"

"Yes, she did all that I could have hoped for," said Tom. "Now for the next test."

"Bless my collar button! is there another?"

"Just down into a trench and out again." Tom said. "This is comparatively simple. It's only what she'll have to do every day in Flanders."

The tank waddled on. A duck's sidewise walk is about the only kind of motion that can be compared to it. The going was easier now, for it was across a big field, and Tom told his friends that at the other end was a deep, steep and rocky ravine in which he had decided to give the tank another test.

"We'll imagine that ravine is a trench," he said, "and that we've got to get on the other side of it. Of course, we won't be under fire, as the tanks will be at the front, but aside from that the test will be just as severe."

A little later Tank A brought her occupants to the edge of the "trench."

"Now, little girl," cried Tom exultingly, patting the rough steel side of his tank, "show them what you can do!"

"Bless my plum pudding!" cried Mr. Damon, "are you really going down there, Tom Swift?"

"I am," answered the young inventor. "It won't be dangerous. We'll crawl down and crawl out. Hold fast!"

He steered the machine straight for the edge of the ravine, and as the nose slipped over and the broad steel belts bit into the earth the tank tilted downward at a sickening angle.

She appeared to be making the descent safely, when there was a sudden change. The earth seemed to slip out from under the broad caterpillar belts, and then the tank moved more rapidly.

"Tom, we're turning over!" shouted Ned. "We're capsizing!"

Chapter XIV
The Ruined Factory

Only too true were the words Ned Newton shouted to his chum. Tank A was really capsizing. She had advanced to the edge of the gully and started down it, moving slowly on the caterpillar bands of steel. Then had come a sudden lurch, caused, as they learned afterward, by the slipping off of a great quantity of shale from an underlying shelf of rock.

This made unstable footing for the tank. One side sank lower than the other, and before Tom could neutralize this by speeding up one motor and slowing down the other the tank slowly turned over on its side.

"But she isn't going to stop here!" cried Ned, as he found himself thrown about like a pill in a box. "We're going all the way over!"

"Let her go over!" cried Tom, not that he could stop the tank now. "It won't hurt her. She's built for just this sort of thing!"

And over Tank A did go. Over and over she rolled, sidewise, tumbling and sliding down the shale sides of the great gully.

"Hold fast! Grab the rings!" cried Tom to his two companions in the tower with him. "That's what they're for!"

Ned and Mr. Damon understood. In fact, the latter had already done as Tom suggested. The young inventor had read that the British tanks frequently turned turtle, and he had this in mind when he made provision in his own for the safety of passengers and crew.

As soon as he felt the tank careening, Tom had pressed the signal ordering the motors stopped, and now only the force of gravity was operating. But that was sufficient to carry the big machine to the bottom of the gulch, whither she slid with a great cloud of sand, shale and dust.

"Bless my—bless my—" Mr. Damon was murmuring, but he was so flopped about, tossed from one side to the other, and it took so much of his attention and strength to hold on to the safety ring, that he could not properly give vent; to one of his favorite expressions.

But there comes an end to all things, even to the descent of a tank, and Tom's big machine soon stopped rolling, sliding, and turning improvised somersaults, and rested in a pile of soft shale at the bottom of the gully. And the tank was resting on her back!

"We've turned turtle!" cried Ned, as he noted that he was standing on what, before, had been the ceiling of the observation tower. But as everything was of steel, and as there was no movable furniture, no great harm was done. In fact, one could as well walk on the ceiling of the tank as on the floor.

"But how are you going to get her right side up?" asked Mr. Damon.

"Oh, turning upside down is only one of the stunts of the game. I can right her," was the answer.

"How?" asked Ned.

"Well, she'll right herself if there's ground enough for the steel belts to get a grip on."

"But can the motors work upside down?"

"They surely can!" responded Tom. "I made 'em that way on purpose. The gasolene feeds by air pressure, and that works standing on its head, as well as any other way. It's going to be a bit awkward for the men to operate the controls, but we won't be this way long. Before I start to right her, though, I want to make sure nothing is broken."

Tom signaled to the engine room, and, as the power was off and the speaking tube could be used, he called through it:

"How are you down there?"

"Right-o!" came back the answer from a little Englishman Tom had hired because he knew something about the British tanks. "'Twas a bit of nastiness for a while, but it won't take us long to get up ag'in."

"That's good!" commented Tom. "I'll come down and have a look at you."

It was no easy matter, with the tank capsized, to get to the main engine room, but Tom Swift managed it. To his delight, aside from a small break in one of the minor machines, which would not interfere with the operation or motive force of the monster war engine, everything was in good shape. There was no leak from the gasolene tanks, which was one of the contingencies Tom feared, and, as he had said, the motors would work upside down as well as right side up, a fact he had proved more than once in his Hawk.

"Well, we'll make a start," he told his chief engineer. "Stand by when I give the signal, and we'll try to crawl out of this right side up."

"How are you going to do it?" asked Ned, as his chum crawled back into the observation tower.

"Well, I'm going to run her part way up the very steepest part of the ravine I can find—the side of a house would do as well if it could stand the strain. I'm going to stand the tank right up on her nose, so to speak, and tip her over so she'll come right again."

Slowly the tank started off, while Tom and his friends in the observation tower anxiously awaited the result of the novel progress. Ned and Mr. Damon clung to the safety rings. Tom put his arm through one and hung on grimly, while he used both hands on the steering apparatus and the controls.

Of course the trailer wheels were useless in a case of this kind, and the tank had to be guided by the two belts run at varying speeds.

"Here we go!" cried Tom, and the tank started. It was a queer sensation to be moving upside down, but it did not last very long. Tom steered the tank straight at the opposite wall of the ravine, where it rose steeply. One of the broad belts ran up on that side. The other was revolved in the opposite direction. Up and up, at a sickening angle, went Tank A.

Slowly the tank careened, turning completely over on her longer axis, until, as Tom shut off the power, he and his friends once more found themselves standing where they belonged—on the floor of the observation tower.

"Right side up with care!" quoted Ned, with a laugh. "Well, that was some stunt—believe me!"

"Bless my corn plaster, I should say so!" cried Mr. Damon.

"Well, I'm glad it happened," commented Tom. "It showed what she can do when she's put to it. Now we'll get out of this ditch."

Slowly the tank lumbered along, proper side up now, the men in the motor room reporting that everything was all right, and that with the exception of a slight unimportant break, no damage had been done.

Straight for the opposite steep side of the gully Tom directed his strange craft, and at a point where the wall of the gulch gave a good footing for the steel belts, Tank A pulled herself out and up to level ground.

"Well, I'm glad that's over," remarked Ned, with a sigh of relief, as the tank waddled along a straight stretch. "And to think of having to do that same thing under heavy fire!"

"That's part of the game," remarked Tom. "And don't forget that we can fire, too—or we'll be able to when I get the guns in place. They'll help to balance the machine better, too, and render her less likely to overturn."

Tom considered the test a satisfactory one and, a little later, guided his tank back to the shop, where men were set to work repairing the little damage done and making some adjustments.

"What's next on the program?" asked Ned of his chum one day about a week later. "Any more tests in view?"

"Yes," answered Tom. "I've got the machine guns in place now. We are going to try them out and also endeavor to demolish a building and some barbed wire. Like to come along?"

"I would!" cried Ned.

A little later the tank was making her way over a field. Tom pointed toward a deserted factory, which had long been partly in ruins, but some of the walls of which still stood.

"I'm going to bombard that," he announced, and then try to batter it down and roll over it like a Juggernaut. Are you game?"

"Do your worst!" laughed Ned. "Let me man one of the machine guns!"

"All right," agreed Tom. "Concentrate your fire. Make believe you're going against the Germans!"

Slowly, but with resistless energy, the tank approached the ruined factory.

"Are you sure there's no one in it, Tom?"

"Sure! Blaze away!"

Chapter XV
Across Country

Ned Newton sighted his machine gun. Tom had showed him how to work it, and indeed the young bank clerk had had some practice with a weapon like this, erected on a stationary tripod. But this was the first time Ned had attempted to fire from the tank while it was moving, and he found it an altogether different matter.

"Say, it sure is hard to aim where you want to!" he shouted across to Tom, it being necessary, even in the conning tower, where this one gun was mounted, to speak loudly to make one's self heard above the hum, the roar and rattle of the machinery in the interior of Tank A, and below and to the rear of the two young men.

"Well, that's part of the game," Tom answered. "I'm sending her along over as smooth ground as I can pick out, but it's rough at best. Still this is nothing to what you'll get in Flanders."

"If I get there!" exclaimed Ned grimly. "Well, here goes!" and once more he tried to aim the machine gun at the middle of the brick wall of the ruined factory.

A moment later there was a rattle and a roar as the quick-firing mechanism started, and a veritable hail of bullets swept out at the masonry. Tom and Ned could see where they struck, knocking off bits of stone, brick and cement.

"Sweep it, Ned! Sweep it!" cried Tom. "Imagine a crowd of Germans are charging out at you, and sweep 'em out of the way!"

Obeying this command, the young man moved the barrel of the machine gun from side to side and slightly up and down. The effect was at once apparent. The wall showed spatter-marks of the bullets over a wider area, and had a body of Teutons been before the factory, or even inside it, many of them would have been accounted for, since there were several holes in the wall through which Ned's bullets sped, carrying potential death with them.

"That's better!" shouted Tom. "That'll do the business! Now I'm going to open her up, Ned!"

"Open her up?" cried the young bank clerk, as he ceased firing.

"Yes; crack the wall of that factory as I would a nut! Watch me take it on high—that is, if the old tank doesn't go back on me!"

"You mean you're going to ride right over that building, Tom?"

"I mean I'm going to try! If Tank A does as I expect her to, she'll butt into that wall, crush it down by force and weight, and then waddle over the ruins. Watch!"

Tom sent some signals to the motor room. At once there was noticed an increase in the vibrations of the ponderous machine.

"They're giving her more speed," said Tom. "And I guess we'll need it."

Straight for the old factory went Tank A. In spite of its ruined condition, some of the walls were still firm, and seemed to offer a big obstacle to even so powerful an engine of war as this monstrous tank.

"Get ready now, Ned," Tom advised. "And when I crack her open for you cut loose with the machine gun again. This gun is supposed to fire straight ahead and a little to either side. There are other guns at left and right, amidships, as I might say, and there's also one in the stern, to take care of any attack from that direction.

"The men in charge of them will fire at the same time you do, and it will be as near like a real attack as we can make it—with the exception of not being fired back at. And I wouldn't mind if such were the case, for I don't believe anything, outside of heavy artillery, will have any effect on this tank."

Tank A was now almost at her maximum speed as she approached closer to the deserted factory. Ned and Tom, in the conning tower, saw the largest of the remaining walls looming before them. Straight at it rushed the ponderous machine, and the next moment there came a shock which almost threw Ned away from his gun and back against the steel wall behind him.

"Hold fast!" cried Tom. "Here we go! Fire. Ned! Fire!"

There was a crash as the blunt nose of the great war tank hit the wall and crumpled it up.

A great hole was made in the masonry, and what was not crushed under the caterpillar belts of the tank fell in a shower of bricks, stone and cement on top of the machine.

Like a great hail storm the broken masonry pelted the steel sides and top of the tank. But she felt them no more than does an alligator the attacks of a colony of ants. Right on through the dust the tank crushed her way. Added to the noise of the falling walls was that of the machine guns, which were barking away like a kennel of angry hounds eager to be unleashed at the quarry.

Ned kept his gun going until the heat of it warned him to stop and let the barrel cool, or he knew he would jam some of the mechanism. The other guns were firing, too, and the bullets sent up little spatter points of dust as they hit.

"Great jumping hoptoads!" yelled Ned above the riot of racket outside and inside. "Feel her go, Tom!"

"Yes, she's just chewing it up, all right!" cried the young inventor, his eyes shining with delight.

The tank had actually burst her way through the solid wall of the old factory, permission to complete the demolition of which Tom had secured from the owners. Then the great machine kept right on. She fairly "walked" over the piles of masonry, dipped down into what had been a basement, now partly filled with debris, and kept on toward another wall.

"I'm going through that, too!" cried Tom.

And he did, knocking it down and sending his tank over the piled-up ruins, while the machine guns barked, coughed and spluttered, as Ned and the others inside the tank held back the firing levers.

Right through the opposite wall, as through the one she had already demolished, the tank careened on her way, to emerge, rather battered and dust-covered, on the other side of what was left of the factory. And there was not much of it left. Tank A had well-nigh completed its demolition.

"If there'd been a nest of Germans in there," said Tom, as he brought the machine to a stop in a field beyond the factory, "they'd have gotten out in a hurry."

"Or taken the consequences," added Ned, as he wiped the sweat from his powder-blackened and oil-smeared face. "I certainly kept my gun going."

"Yes, and so did the others," reported one of the mechanics, as he emerged from the "cubby hole," where the great motors had now ceased their hum and roar.

"How'd she stand it?" asked Tom.

"All right inside," answered the man. "I was wondering how she looks from the outside."

"Oh, it would take more than that to damage her," said Tom, with pardonable pride. "That was pie for her! Solid concrete, which she may have to chew up on the Western front, may present another kind of problem, but I guess she'll be able to master that too. Well, let's have a look."

He and Ned, with some of the crew and gunners, went outside the tank. She was a sorry-looking sight, very different from the trim appearance she had presented when she first left the shop. Bricks, bits of stone, and piles of broken cement in chunks and dust lay thick on her broad back. But no real damage had been done, as a hasty examination showed.

"Well, are you satisfied, Tom?" asked his chum.

"Yes, and more," was the answer. "Of course this wasn't the hardest test to which she could have been submitted, but it will do to show what punishment she can stand. Being shot at from big guns is another matter. I'll have to wait until she gets to Flanders to see what effect that will have. But I know the kind of armor skin she has, and that doesn't worry me. There's one thing more I want to do while I have her out now."

"What's that?" asked Ned.

"Take her for a long trip cross country, and then shove her through some extra heavy barbed wire. I'm certain she'll chew that up, but I want to see it actually done. So now, if you want to come along, Ned, we'll go cross country."

"I'm with you!"

"Get inside then. We'll let the dust and masonry blow and rattle off as we go along."

The tank started off across the fields, which stretched for many miles on either side of the deserted factory, when suddenly Ned, who was again at his post in the observation tower, called:

"Look, Tom!"

"What at?"

"That corner of the factory which is still standing. Look at those men coming out and running away!"

Ned pointed, and his chum, leaning over from the steering wheel and controls, gave a start of surprise as he saw three figures clambering down over the broken debris and making their way out of what had once been a doorway.

"Did they come out of the factory, Ned?"

"They surely did! And unless I miss my guess they were in it, or around it, when we went through like a fellow carrying the football over the line for a touchdown."

"In there when the tank broke open things?"

"I think so. I didn't see them before, but they certainly ran out as we started away."

"This has got to be looked into!" decided Tom. "Come on, Ned! It may be more of that spy business!"

Tom Swift stopped the tank and prepared to get out.

Chapter XVI
The Old Barn

"There's no use chasing after 'em, Tom," observed Ned, as the two chums stood side by side outside the tank and gazed after the three men running off across the fields as fast as they could go. "They've got too much a start of us."

"I guess you're right, Ned," agreed Tom. "And we can't very well pursue them in the tank. She goes a bit faster than anything of her build, but a running man is more than a match for her in a short distance. If I had the Hawk here, there'd be a different story to tell."

"Well, seeing that you haven't," replied Ned, "suppose we let them go—which we'll have to, whether we want to or not—and see where they were hiding and if they left any traces behind."

"That's a good idea," returned Tom.

The place whence the men had emerged was a portion of the old factory farthest removed from the walls the tank had crunched its way through. Consequently, that part was the least damaged.

Tom and Ned came to what seemed to have been the office of the building when the factory was in operation. A door, from which most of the glass had been broken, hung on one hinge, and, pushing this open, the two chums found themselves in a room that bore evidences of having been the bookkeeper's department. There were the remains of cabinet files, and a broken letter press, while in one corner stood a safe.

"Maybe they were cracking that," said Ned.

"They were wasting their time if they were," observed Tom, "for the combination is broken—any one can open it," and he demonstrated this by swinging back one of the heavy doors.

A quantity of papers fell out, or what had been papers, for they were now torn and the edges charred, as if by some recent fire.

"They were burning these!" cried Ned. "You can smell the smoke yet. They came here to destroy some papers, and we surprised them!"

"I believe you're right," agreed Tom. "The ashes are still warm." And he tested them with his hand. "They wanted to destroy something, and when they found we were here they clapped the blazing stuff into the safe, thinking it would burn there.

"But the closing of the doors cut off the supply of air and the fire smouldered and went out. It burned enough so that it didn't leave us very much in the way of evidence, though," went on Tom ruefully, as he poked among the charred scraps.

"Maybe you can read some of 'em," suggested Ned.

"Part of the writing is in German," Tom said, as he looked over the mass. "I don't believe it would be worth while to try it. Still, I can save it. Here, I'll sweep the stuff into a box, and if we get a chance we can try to patch it together," and finding a broken box in what had been the factory office the young inventor managed to get into it the charred remains of the papers.

A further search failed to reveal anything that would be useful in the way of evidence to determine what object the three men could have had in hiding in the ruins, and Tom and Ned returned to the tank.

"What do you think about them, Tom?" asked Ned, as they were about to start off once more for the cross-country test.

"Well, it seems like a silly thing to say—as if I imagined my tank was all there was in this part of the country to make trouble—but I believe those men had some connection with Simpson and with that spy Schwen!"

"I agree with you!" exclaimed Ned. "And I think if we could get head or tail of those burned papers we'd find that there was some correspondence there between the man I saw up the tree and the workman you had arrested."

"Too bad we weren't a bit quicker," commented Tom. "They must have been in the factory when we charged it—probably came there to be in seclusion while they talked, plotted and planned. They must have been afraid to go out when the tank was walking through the walls."

"I guess that's it," agreed Ned. "Did you recognize any of the men, Tom?"

"No, I didn't see 'em as soon as you did, and when they were running they had their backs toward me. Was Simpson one?"

"I can't be sure. If one was, I guess he'll think we are keeping pretty closely after him, and he may give this part of the country a wide berth."

"I hope he does," returned Tom. "Do you know, Ned, I have an idea that these fellows—Schwen Simpson, and those back of them, including Blakeson—are trying to get hold of the secret of my tank for the Germans."

"I shouldn't be surprised. But you've got it finished now, haven't you? They can't get your patents away from you."

"No, it isn't that," said Tom. "There are certain secrets about the mechanism of the tank—the way I've increased the speed and power, the use of the spanners, and things like that—which would be useful for the Germans to know. I wouldn't want them to find out these secrets, and they could do that if they were in the tank a while, or had her in their possession."

"They couldn't do that, Tom—get possession of her—could they?"

"There's no telling. I'm going to be doubly on the watch. That fellow Blakeson is in the pay of the plotters, I believe. He has a big machine shop, and he might try to duplicate my tank if he knew how she was made inside."

"I see! That's why he was inquiring about a good machinist, I suppose, though he'll be mightily surprised when he learns it was you he was talking to the time your Hawk met with the little mishap."

"Yes, I guess maybe he will be a bit startled," agreed Tom. "But I haven't seen him around lately, and maybe he has given up."

"Don't trust to that!" warned Ned.

The tank was now progressing easily along over fields, hesitating not at small or big ditches, flow going uphill and now down, across a stretch of country thinly settled, where even fences were a rarity. When they came to wooden ones Tom had the workmen get out and take down the bars. Of course the tank could have crushed them like toothpicks, but Tom was mindful of the rights of farmers, and a broken fence might mean strayed cows, or the letting of cattle into a field of grain or corn, to the damage of both cattle and fodder.

"There's a barbed-wire fence," observed Ned, as he pointed to one off some distance across the field. "Why don't you try demolishing that?"

"Oh, it would be too easy! Besides, I don't want the bother of putting it up again. When I make the barbed-wire test I want some set up on heavy posts, and with many strands, as it is in Flanders. Even that won't stop the tank, but I'm anxious to see how she breaks up the wire and supports—just what sort of a breach she makes. But I have a different plan in mind now.

"I'm going to try to find a wooden building we can charge as we did the masonry factory. I want to smash up a barn, and I'll have to pick out an old one for choice, for in these war days we must conserve all we can, even old barns."

"What's the idea of using a barn, Tom?"

"Well, I want to test the tank under all sorts of conditions—the same conditions she'll meet with on the Western front. We've proved that a brick and stone factory is no obstacle."

"Then how could a flimsy wooden barn be?"

"Well, that's just it. I don't think that it will, but it may be that a barn when smashed will get tangled up in the endless steel belts, and clog them so they'll jam. That's the reason I want to try a wooden structure next."

"Do you know where to find one?"

"Yes; about a mile from here is one I've had my eyes on ever since I began constructing the tank. I don't know who owns it, but it's such a ramshackle affair that he can't object to having it knocked into kindling wood for him. If he does holler, I can pay him for the damage done. So now for a barn, Ned, unless you're getting tired and want to go back?"

"I should say not! Speaking of barns, I'm with you till the cows come home! Want any more machine gun work?"

"No, I guess not. This barn isn't particularly isolated, and the shooting might scare horses and cattle. We can smash things up without the guns."

The tank was going on smoothly when suddenly there was a lurch to one side, and the great machine quickly swung about in a circle.

"Hello!" cried Ned. "What's up now? Some new stunt?"

"Must be something wrong," answered the young inventor. "One of the belts has stopped working. That's why we're going in a circle."

He shut off the power and hastened down to the motor room. There he found his men gathered about one of the machines.

"What's wrong?" asked Tom quickly.

"Just a little accident," replied the head machinist. "One of the boys dropped his monkey wrench and it smashed some spark plugs. That caused a short circuit and the left hand motor went out of business. We'll have her fixed in a jiffy."

Tom looked relieved, and the machinist was as good as his word. In a few minutes the tank was moving forward again. It crossed out to the road, to the great astonishment of some farmers, and the fright of their horses, and then Tom once more swung her into the fields.

"There's the old barn I spoke of," he remarked to Ned. "It's almost as bad a ruin as the factory was. But we'll have a go at it."

"Going to smash it?" asked Ned.

"I'm going right through it!" Tom cried.

Chapter XVII
Veiled Threats

Like some prehistoric monster about to charge down upon another of its kind, Tank A, under the guidance of Tom Swift, reeled and bumped her way over the uneven fields toward the old barn. Within the monster of steel and iron were raucous noises: the clang and clatter of the powerful gasolene motors; the rattle of the wheels and gears; all making so much noise that, in the engine room proper, not a word could be heard. Every order had to be given by signs, and Tom sent his electric signals from the conning tower in the same way. When running at full speed, it was almost impossible, even in the tower, which was some distance removed from the engine room, to hear voices unless the words were shouted.

"Why don't you go at it?" cried Ned to his "friend, who was peering through the observation slot in the tower."

"I'm getting in good position," Tom answered. "Or rather, the worst position I can find. I want to give the tank a good try-out, and I'm going at the barn on the assumption that this is in enemy country and that I can't pick and choose my advance.

"So I want to come up through that gully, and go at the barn from the long way. That will be the worst possible way I could do it, and if old Tank A stands the gaff I'll know she's a little bit nearer all right."

"I think she's all right as she is!" asserted Ned in a yell, for just then Tom signaled for more speed, and the consequent increase in the rattling and banging noises made it correspondingly difficult for talk to be heard.

The big machine now tipped into the little gully spoken of by Tom. This meant a dip downward, and then a climb out again and an attack on the barn going uphill and at an angle. But, as the young inventor had said, it would make a severe test and that was what he wanted to give his ponderous machine.

Ned grasped one of the safety rings, as, with a reel to one side, almost as if it were going to capsize, the tank rumbled on. Tom cast a half-amused smile at his chum, and then threw over the guiding lever.

The tank rolled down into the gully. It was rough and filled with stones and boulders, some of considerable size. But Tank A made less than nothing even of the largest rocks. Some she crushed beneath her steel belts. Others she simply "walked" over, smashing them down into the soil.

Now the big machine reached the bottom of the gulch and started up the sides, which, though not as steep as the trench in which she had capsized, still were not easy going.

"Now for it!" cried Tom, as he signaled for full speed.

Up climbed the tank. Now she was halfway. A moment later, and she was at the top, and then a forward careening motion told that she had passed over the summit and was ready for the attack proper.

Ned gave a quick glance through the slot nearest him. He had a glimpse of the barn, and then he saw something else. This was the sight of a man running away from the dilapidated structure—a man who glanced toward the tank with a face that showed great fright.

"Stop! Stop!" yelled Ned. "There may be folks in there, Tom! I just saw a man run out!"

"All right!" Tom cried, though Ned could hardly hear him. "Tell me when we get on the other side! We're going through now!"

"But," shouted Ned, "don't you understand? I saw a man come out of there! Maybe there's more inside! Wait, Tom, and—"

But it was too late. The next instant there was a smashing, grinding, splintering crash, a noise as of a thunder-clap, and Tank A fairly ate her way through the old barn as a rat might eat his way into a soft cheese, only infinitely more quickly.

On and on and through and through went the tank, knocking beams, boards, rafters and timbers hither and thither. Minding not at all the weight of great beams on her back, caring nothing for those that got in the way of her steel belts, heeding not the wall of wood that reared itself before her in a barrier of splinters and slivers, Tank A went on and on until finally, with another grinding crash, as she smashed her way through the farthermost wall, the great engine of war emerged on the other side and came panting into the field, dragging with her a part of the structure clinging to her steel sides.

"Well," cried Tom, with a laugh, as he signaled for the power to be shut off, thereby making it possible for ordinary conversation to be heard, "I guess we didn't do a thing to that barn!"

"Not much left of it, for a fact, Tom," agreed Ned, as he looked through the after observation slots at the ruin in the rear. "But didn't you hear what I was saying?"

"I heard you yelling something to me, but I was too anxious to go at it as fast as I could. I didn't want to stop then. What was the trouble?"

"That's what I'm afraid of, Tom—there may be trouble. Just before you tackled the barn for a knockdown, instead of a touchdown, as we might say, I saw a man running out of it. I thought if there was one there, perhaps there might be more. That's why I yelled to you."

"A man running from the old barn!" cried Tom. "Whew!" he whistled. "I wish I had seen him. But, Ned, if one ran out of harm's way, any others who might possibly be in there would do the same thing, wouldn't they?"

"I hope so," returned Ned doubtfully.

"Great Scott!" cried Tom, as the possibility was borne home to him. "If anything has happened—"

He sprang for the door of the tower and threw over the catch, springing out, followed by Ned. From the engine room of the armored tank the men came, smiles of gratification on their faces.

"We certainly busted her wide open, Mr. Swift!" called the chief mechanician.

"Yes," assented the young inventor; but there was not as much gratification in his voice as there should have been. "There isn't much of a barn left, but Ned thinks he saw some one run out, and if there was one man there may have been more. We'd better have a look around, I guess."

The engineering force exchanged glances. Then Hank Baldwin, who was in charge of the motors, said:

"Well, if there was anybody in that barn when we chewed her up I wouldn't give much for his hide, German or not."

"Let us hope no one was in there," murmured Tom.

They turned to go back to the demolished structure, fear and worry in their hearts. No more complete ruin could be imagined. If a cyclone had swept over the barn it could not have more certainly leveled it. And, not only was it leveled, crushed down in the center by the great weight of the tank, but the boards and beams were broken into small pieces. Parts of them clung in long, grotesque splinters to the endless steel belts.

"I don't see how we're going to find anybody if he's in there," remarked Hank.

"We'll have to," insisted Tom. "We can look about and call. If any one is there he may have been off to one side or to one end, and be protected under the debris. I wish I had heard you call, Ned."

"I wish you had, Tom. I yelled for all I was worth."

"I know you did. I was too eager to go on, and, at the same time, I really couldn't stop well on that hill. I had to keep on going. Well, now to learn the worst!"

They walked back toward the demolished barn. But they had not reached it when from around the corner swung a big automobile. In it were several men, but chief, in vision at least, among them, was a burly farmer who had a long, old-fashioned gun in his hands. On his bearded face was a grim look as he leaped out before the machine had fairly stopped, and called:

"Hold on, there! I guess you've done damage enough! Now you can pay for it or take the consequences!" And he motioned to Tom, Ned, and the others to halt.

Chapter XVIII
Ready for France

Such was the reaction following the crashing through of the barn, coupled with the sudden appearance of the men in the automobile and the threat of the farmer, that, for the moment, Tom, Ned, or their companions from the tank could say nothing. They just stood staring at the farmer with the gun, while he grimly regarded them. It was Tom who spoke first.

"What's the idea?" asked the young inventor. "Why don't you want us to look through the ruins?"

"You'll learn soon enough!" was the grim answer.

But Tom was not to be put off with undecided talk.

"If there's been an accident," he said, "we're sorry for it. But delay may be dangerous. If some one is hurt—"

"You'll be hurt, if I have my way about it!" snapped the farmer, "and hurt in a place where it always tells. I mean your pocketbook! That's the kind of a man I am—practical."

"He means if we've killed or injured any one we'll have to pay damages," whispered Ned to Tom. "But don't agree to anything until you see your lawyer. That's a hot one, though, trying to claim damages before he knows who's hurt!"

"I've got to find out more about this," Tom answered. He started to walk on.

"No you don't!" cried the farmer, with a snarl. "As I said, you folks has done damage enough with your threshing machine, or whatever you call it. Now you've got to pay!"

"We are willing to," said Tom, as courteously as he could. "But first we want to know who has been hurt, or possibly killed. Don't you think it best to get them to a doctor, and then talk about money damages later?"

"Doctor? Hurt?" cried the farmer, the other men in the auto saying nothing. "Who said anything about that?"

"I thought," began Tom, "that you—"

"I'm talkin' about damages to my barn!" cried the farmer. "You had no right to go smashing it up this way, and you've got to pay for it, or my name ain't Amos Kanker!"

"Oh!" and there was great relief in Tom's voice. "Then we haven't killed any one?"

"I don't know what you've done," answered the farmer, and his voice was not a pleasant one. "I'm sure I can't keep track of all your ructions. All I know is that you've ruined my barn, and you've got to pay for it, and pay good, too!"

"For that old ramshackle?" cried Ned.

"Hush!" begged Tom, in a low voice. "I'm willing to pay, Ned, for the sake of having proved what my tank could do. I'm only too glad to learn no one was hurt. Was there?" he asked, turning to the farmer.

"Was there what?"

"Was there anybody in your barn?"

"Not as I knows on," was the grouchy answer. "A man who saw your machine coming thought she was headed for my building, and he run and told me. Then some friends of mine brought me here in their machine. I tell you I've got all the evidence I need ag'in you, an' I'm going to have damages! That barn was worth three thousand dollars if it was worth a cent, and—"

"This matter can easily be settled," said Tom, trying to keep his temper. "My name is Swift, and—"

"Don't get swift with me, that's all I ask!" and the farmer laughed grimly at his clumsy joke.

"I'll do whatever is right," Tom said, with dignity. "I live over near Shopton, and if you want to send your lawyer to see mine, why—"

"I don't believe in lawyers!" broke in the farmer. "All they think of is to get what they can for theirselves. And I can do that myself. I'll get it out of you before you leave, or, anyhow, before you take your contraption away," and he glanced at the tank.

The same suspicion came at once to Tom and Ned, and the latter gave voice to it when he murmured in a low voice to his chum:

"This is a frame-up—a scheme, Tom. He doesn't care a rap for the barn. It's some of that Blakeson's doing, to make trouble for you."

"I believe you!" agreed Tom. "Now I know what to do."

He looked toward the collapsed barn, as if making a mental computation of its value, and then turned toward the farmer.

"I'm very sorry," said Tom, "if I have caused any trouble. I wanted to test my machine out on a wooden structure, and I picked your barn. I suppose I should have come to you first, but I did not want to waste time. I saw the barn was of practically no value."

"No value!" broke in the farmer. "Well, I'll show you, young man, that you can't play fast and loose with other people's property and not settle!"

"I'm perfectly willing to, Mr. Kanker. I could see that the barn was almost ready to fall, and I had already determined, before sending my tank through it, to pay the owner any reasonable sum. I am willing to do that now."

"Well, of course if you're so ready to do that," replied the farmer, and Ned thought he caught a glance pass between him and one of the men in the auto, "if you're ready to do that, just hand over three thousand dollars, and we'll call it a day's work. It's really worth more, but I'll say three thousand for a quick settlement."

"Why, this barn," cried Ned, "isn't worth half that! I know something about real estate values, for our bank makes loans on farms around here—"

"Your bank ain't made me no loans, young man!" snapped Mr. Kanker. "I don't need none. My place is free and clear! And three thousand dollars is the price of my barn you've knocked to smithereens. If you don't want to pay, I'll find a way to make you. And I'll hold you, or your tank, as you call it, security for my damages! You can take your choice about that."

"You can't hold us!" cried Tom. "Such things aren't done here!"

"Well, then, I'll hold your tank!" cried the farmer. "I guess it'll sell for pretty nigh onto what you owe me, though what it's good for I can't see. So you pay me three thousand dollars or leave your machine here as security."

"That's the game!" whispered Ned. "There's some plot here. They want to get possession of your tank, Tom, and they've seized on this chance to do it."

"I believe you," agreed the young inventor. "Well, they'll find that two can play at that game. Mr. Kanker," he went on, "it is out of the question to claim your barn is worth three thousand dollars."

"Oh, is it?" sneered the farmer. "Well, I didn't ask you to come here and make kindling wood of it! That was your doings, and you've had your fun out of it. Now you can pay the piper, and I'm here to make you pay!" And he brought the gun around in a menacing manner.

"He's right, in a way," said Ned to his chum. "We should have secured his permission first. He's got us in a corner, and almost any jury of farmers around here, after they heard the story of the smashed barn, would give him heavy damages. It isn't so much that the barn is worth that as it is his property rights that we've violated. A farmer's barn is his castle, so to speak."

"I guess you're right," agreed Tom, with a rather rueful face. "But I'm not going to hand him over three thousand dollars. In fact, I haven't that much with me."

"Oh, well, I don't suppose he'd want it all in cash."

But, it appeared, that was just what the farmer wanted. He went over all his arguments again, and it could not be denied that he had the law on his side. As he rightly said, Tom could not expect to go about the country, "smashing up barns and such like," without being willing to pay.

"Well, what you going to do?" asked the farmer at last. "I can't stay here all day. I've got work to do. I can't go around smashing barns. I want three thousand dollars, or I'll hold your contraption for security."

This last he announced with more conviction after he had had a talk with one of the men in the automobile. And it was this consultation that confirmed Tom and Ned in their belief that the whole thing was a plot, growing out of Tom's rather reckless destruction of the barn; a plot on the part of Blakeson and his gang. That they had so speedily taken advantage of this situation carelessly given them was only another evidence of how closely they were on Tom's trail.

"That man who ran out of the barn must have been the same one who was in the factory," whispered Ned to his chum. "He probably saw us coming this way and ran on ahead to have the farmer all primed in readiness. Maybe he knew you had planned to ram the barn."

"Maybe he did. I've had it in mind for some time, and spoken to some of my men about it."

"More traitors in camp, then, I'm afraid, Tom. We'll have to do some more detective work. But let's get this thing settled. He only wants to hold your tank, and that will give the man, into whose hands he's playing, a chance to inspect her."

"I believe you. But if I have to leave her here I'll leave some men on guard inside. It won't be any worse than being stalled in No Man's Land. In fact, it won't be so bad. But I'll do that rather than be gouged."

"No, Tom, you won't. If you did leave some one on guard, there'd be too much chance of their getting the best of him. You must take your tank away with you."

"But how can I? I can't put up three thousand dollars in cash, and he says he won't take a check for fear I'll stop payment. I see his game, but I don't see how to block it."

"But I do!" cried Ned.

"What!" exclaimed Tom. "You don't mean to say, even if you do work in a bank, that you've got three thousand in cash concealed about your person, do you?"

"Pretty nearly, Tom, or what is just as good. I have that amount in Liberty Bonds. I was going to deliver them to a customer who has ordered them but not paid for them. They are charged up against me at the bank, but I'm good for that, I guess. Now I'll loan you these bonds, and you can give them to this cranky old farmer as security for damages. Mind, don't make them as a payment. They're simply security—the same as when an autoist leaves his car as bail. Only we don't want to leave our car, we'd rather have it with us," and he looked over at the tank, bristling with splinters from the demolished barn.

"Well, I guess that's the only way out," said Tom. "Lucky you had those bonds with you. I'll take them, and give you a receipt for them. In fact, I'll buy them from you and let the farmer hold them as security."

And this, eventually, was done. After much hemming and hawing and consultation with the men in the automobile, Mr. Kanker said he would accept the bonds. It was made clear that they were not in payment of any damages, though Tom admitted he was liable for some, but that Uncle Sam's war securities were only a sort of bail, given to indicate that, some time later, when a jury had passed on the matter, the young inventor would pay Mr. Kanker whatever sum was agreed upon as just.

"And now," said Tom, as politely as he could under the circumstances, "I suppose we will be allowed to depart."

"Yes, take your old shebang offen my property!" ordered Mr. Kanker, with no very good grace. "And if you go knocking down any more barns, I'll double the price on you!"

"I guess he's a bit roiled because he couldn't hold the tank," observed Ned to Tom, as they walked together to the big machine. "His friends—our enemies—evidently hoped that was what could be done. They want to get at some of the secrets."

"I suppose so," conceded Tom. "Well, we're out of that, and I've proved all I want to."

"But I haven't—quite," said Ned.

"What's missing?" asked his chum, as they got back in the tank.

"Well, I'd like to make sure that the fellow who ran from the factory was the same one I saw sneaking out of the barn. I believe he was, and I believe that Simpson's crowd engineered this whole thing."

"I believe so, too," Tom agreed. "The next thing is to prove it. But that will keep until later. The main thing is we've got our tank, and now I'm going to get her ready for France."

"Will she be in shape to ship soon?" asked Ned.

"Yes, if nothing more happens. I've got a few little changes and adjustments to make, and then she'll be ready for the last test—one of long distance endurance mainly. After that, apart she comes to go to the front, and we'll begin making 'em in quantities here and on the other side."

"Good!" cried Ned. "Down with the Huns!"

Without further incident of moment they went back to the headquarters of the tank, and soon the great machine was safe in the shop where she had been made.

The next two weeks were busy ones for Tom, and in them he put the finishing touches on his machine, gave it a long test over fields and through woods, until finally he announced:

"She's as complete as I can make her! She's ready for France!"

Chapter XIX
Tom is Missing

With Tom Swift's announcement, that his tank was at last ready for real action, came the end of the long nights and days given over on the part of his father, himself, and his men to the development and refinement of the machine, to getting plans and specifications ready so that the tanks could be made quickly and in large numbers in this country and abroad and to the actual building of Tank A. Now all this was done at last, and the first completed tank was ready to be shipped.

Meanwhile the matter of the demolished barn had been left for legal action. Tom and Ned, it developed, had done the proper thing under the circumstances, and they were sure they had foiled at least one plan of the plotters.

"But they won't stop there," declared Ned, who had constituted himself a sort of detective. "They're lying back and waiting for another chance, Tom."

"Well, they won't get it at my tank!" declared the young inventor, with a smile. "I've finished testing her on the road. All I need do now is to run her around this place if I have to; and there won't be much need of that before she's taken apart for shipment. Did you get any trace of Simpson or the men who are with him—Blakeson and the others?"

"No," Ned answered. "I've been nosing around about that farmer, Kanker, but I can't get anything out of him. For all that, I'm sure he was egged on to his hold-up game by some of your enemies. Everything points that way."

"I think you're right," agreed Tom. "Well, we won't bother any more about him. When the trial comes on, I'll pay what the jury says is right. It'll be worth it, for I proved that Tank A can eat up brick, stone or wooden buildings and not get indigestion. That's what I set out to do. So don't worry any more about it, Ned."

"I'm not worrying, but I'd like to get the best of those fellows. The idea of asking three thousand dollars for a shell of a barn!"

"Never mind," replied Tom. "We'll come out all right."

Now that the Liberty Loan drive had somewhat slackened, Ned had more leisure time, and he spent parts of his days and not a few of his evenings at Tom Swift's. Mr. Damon was also a frequent visitor, and he never tired of viewing the tank. Every chance he got, when they tested the big machine in the large field, so well fenced in, the eccentric man was on hand, with his "bless my—!" whatever happened to come most readily to his mind.

Tom, now that his invention was well-nigh perfected, was not so worried about not having the tank seen, even at close range, and the enclosure was not so strictly guarded.

This in a measure was disappointing to Eradicate, who liked the importance of strutting about with a nickel shield pinned to his coat, to show that he was a member of the Swift & Company plant. As for the giant Koku, he really cared little what he did, so long as he pleased Tom, for whom he had an affection that never changed. Koku would as soon sit under a shady tree doing nothing as watch for spies or traitors, of whose identity he was never sure.

So it came that there was not so strict a guard about the place, and Tom and Ned had more time to themselves. Not that the young inventor was not busy, for the details of shipping Tank A to France came to him, as did also the arrangements for making others in this country and planning for the manufacture abroad.

It was one evening, after a particularly hard day's work, when Tom had been making a test in turning the tank in a small space in the enclosed yard, that the two young men were sitting in the machine shop, discussing various matters.

The telephone bell rang, and Ned, being nearest, answered.

"It's for you, Tom," he said, and there was a smile on the face of the young bank clerk.

"Um!" murmured Tom, and he smiled also.

Ned could not repress more smiles as Tom took up the conversation over the wire, and it did not take long for the chum of the youthful inventor to verify his guess that Mary Nestor was at the other end of the instrument.

"Yes, yes," Tom was heard to say. "Why, of course, I'll be glad to come over. Yes, he's here. What? Bring him along? I will if he'll come. Oh, tell him Helen is there! 'Nough said! He'll come, all right!"

And Tom, without troubling to consult his friend, hung up the receiver.

"What's that you're committing me to?" asked Ned.

"Oh, Mary wants us to come over and spend the evening. Helen Sever is there, and they say we can take them downtown if we like."

"I guess we like," laughed Ned. "Come along! We've had enough of musty old problems," for he had been helping Tom in some calculations regarding strength of materials and the weight-bearing power of triangularly constructed girders as compared to the arched variety.

"Yes, I guess it will do us good to get out," and the two friends were soon on their way.

"What's this?" asked Mary, with a laugh, as Tom held out a package tied with pink string. "More dynamite?" she added, referring to an incident which had once greatly perturbed the excitable Mr. Nestor.

"If she doesn't want it, perhaps Helen will take it," suggested Ned, with a twinkle in his eyes. "Halloran said they were just in fresh—"

"Oh, you delightful boy!" cried Helen. "I'm just dying for some chocolates! Let me open them, Mary, if you're afraid of dynamite."

"The only powder in them," said Tom, "is the powdered sugar. That can't blow you up."

And then the young people made merry, Tom, for the time being, forgetting all about his tank.

It was rather late when the two young men strolled back toward the Swift home, Ned walking that way with his chum. Tom started out in the direction of the building where the tank was housed.

"Going to have a good-night look at her?" asked Ned.

"Well, I want to make sure the watchman is on guard. We'll begin taking her apart in a few days, and I don't want anything to happen between now and then."

They walked on toward the big structure, and, as they approached from the side, they were both startled to see a dark shadow—at least so it seemed to the youths—dart away from one of the windows.

"Look!" gasped Ned.

"Hello, there!" cried Tom sharply. "Who's that? Who are you?"

There was no answer, and then the fleeing shadow was merged in the other blackness of the night.

"Maybe it was the watchman making his rounds," suggested Ned.

"No," answered Tom, as he broke into a run. "If it was, he'd have answered. There's something wrong here!"

But he could find nothing when he reached the window from which he and Ned had seen the shadow dart. An examination by means of a pocket electric light betrayed nothing wrong with the sash, and if there were footprints beneath the casement they indicated nothing, for that side of the factory was one frequently used by the workmen.

Tom went into the building, and, for a time, could not find the watchman. When he did come upon the man, he found him rubbing his eyes sleepily, and acting as though he had just awakened from a nap.

"This isn't any way to be on duty!" said Tom sharply. "You're not paid for sleeping!"

"I know it, Mr. Swift," was the apologetic answer. "I don't know what's come over me to-night. I never felt so sleepy in all my life. I had my usual sleep this afternoon, too, and I've drunk strong coffee to keep awake."

"Are you sure you didn't drink anything else?"

"You know I'm a strict temperance man."

"I know you are," said Tom; "but I thought maybe you might have a cold, or something like that."

"No, I haven't taken a thing. I did have a drink of soda water before I came on duty, but that's all."

"Where'd you get it?" asked Tom.

"Well, a man treated me."

"Who?"

"I don't know his name. He met me on the street and asked me how to get to Plowden's hardware store. I showed him—walked part of the way, in fact—and when I left he said he was going to have some soda, and asked me to have some. I did, and it tasted good."

"Well, don't go to sleep again," suggested Tom good-naturedly. "Did you hear anything at the side window a while ago?"

"Not a thing, Mr. Swift. I'll be all right now. I'll take a turn outside in the air."

"All right," assented the young inventor.

Then, as he turned to go into the house and was bidding Ned good-night, Tom said:

"I don't like this."

"What?" asked his chum.

"My sleepy watchman and the figure at the window. I more than half suspect that one of Blakeson's tools followed Kent for the purpose of buying him soda, only I think they might have put a drop or two of chloral in it before he got it. That would make him sleep."

"What are you going to do, Tom?"

"Put another man on guard. If they think they can get into the factory at night, and steal my plans, or get ideas from my tank, I'll fool 'em. I'll have another man on guard."

This Tom did, also telling Koku to sleep in the place, to be ready if called. But there was no disturbance that night, and the next day the work of completing the tank went on with a rush.

It was a day or so after this, and Tom had fixed on it as the time for taking the big machine apart for shipment, that Ned received a telephone message at the bank from Mr. Damon.

"Is Tom Swift over with you?" inquired the eccentric man.

"No. Why?" Ned answered.

"Well, I'm at his shop, and he isn't here. His father says he received a message from you a little while ago, saying to come over in a hurry, and he went. Says you told him to meet you out at that farmer Kanker's place. I thought maybe—"

"At Kanker's place!" cried Ned. "Say, something's wrong, Mr. Damon! Isn't Tom there?"

"No; I'm at his home, and he's been gone for some time. His father supposed he was with you. I thought I would telephone to make sure."

"Whew!" whistled Ned. "There's something doing here, all right, and something wrong! I'll be right over!" he added, as he hung up the receiver.

Chapter XX
The Search

"Haven't you seen anything of him?" asked Mr. Damon, as Ned jumped out of his small runabout at the Swift home as soon as possible after receiving the telephone message that seemed to presage something wrong.

"Seen him? No, certainly not!" answered the young bank clerk. "I'm as much surprised as you are over it. What happened, anyhow?"

"Bless my memorandum pad, but I hardly know!" answered the eccentric man. "I arrived here a little while ago, stopping in merely to pay Tom a visit, as I often do, and he wasn't here. His father was anxiously waiting for him, too, wishing to consult him about some shop matters. Mr. Swift said Tom had gone out with you, or over to your house—I wasn't quite sure which at first—and was expected back any minute.

"Then I called you up," went on Mr. Damon, "and I was surprised to learn you hadn't seen Tom. There must be something wrong, I think."

"I'm sure of it!" exclaimed Ned. "Let's find Mr. Swift. And what's this about his going to meet me over at the place of that farmer, Mr. Kanker, where we had the trouble about the barn Tom demolished?"

"I hardly know, myself. Perhaps Mr. Swift can tell us."

But Mr. Swift was able to throw but little light on Tom's disappearance—whether a natural or forced disappearance remained to be seen.

"No matter where he is, we'll get him," declared Ned. "He hasn't been away a great while, and it may turn out that his absence is perfectly natural."

"And if it's due to the plots of any of his rivals," said Mr. Damon, "I'll denounce them all as traitors, bless my insurance policy, if I don't! And that's what they are! They're playing into the hands of the enemy!"

"All right," said Ned. "But the thing to do now is to get Tom. Perhaps Mrs. Baggert can help us."

It developed that the housekeeper was of more assistance in giving information than was Mr. Swift.

"It was several hours ago," she said, "that the telephone rang and some one asked for Tom. The operator shifted the call to the phone out in the tank shop where he was, and Tom began to talk. The operator, as Tom had instructed her, listened in, as Tom wants always a witness to most matters that go on over his wires of late."

"What did she hear?" asked Ned eagerly.

"She heard what she thought was your voice, I believe," the housekeeper said.

"Me!" cried the young bank clerk. "I haven't talked to Tom to-day, over the phone or any other way. But what next?"

"Well, the operator didn't listen much after that, knowing that any talk between Tom and you was of a nature not to need a witness. Tom hung up and then he came in here, quite excited, and began to get ready to go out."

"What was he excited about?" asked Mr. Damon. "Bless my unlucky stars, but a person ought to keep calm under such circumstances! That's the only way to do! Keep calm! Great Scott! But if I had my way, all those German spies would be—Oh, pshaw! Nothing is too bad for them! It makes my blood boil when I think of what they've done! Tom should have kept cool!"

"Go on. What was Tom excited about?" Ned turned to the housekeeper.

"Well, he said you had called him to tell him to meet you over at that farmer's place," went on Mrs. Baggert. "He said you had some news for him about the men who had tried to get hold of some of his tank secrets, and he was quite worked up over the chance of catching the rascals."

"Whew!" whistled Ned. "This is getting more complicated every minute. There's something deep here, Mr. Damon."

"I agree with you, Ned. And the sooner we find Tom Swift the better. What next, Mrs. Baggert?"

"Well, Tom got ready and went away in his small automobile. He said he'd be back as soon as he could after meeting you."

"And I never said a word to him!" cried Ned. "It's all a plot—a scheme of that Blakeson gang to get him into their power. Oh, how could Tom be so fooled? He knows my voice, over the phone as well as otherwise. I don't see how he could be taken in."

"Let's ask the telephone operator," suggested Mr. Damon. "She knows your voice, too. Perhaps she can give us a clew."

A talk with the young woman at the telephone switchboard in the Swift plant brought out a new point. This was that the speaker, in response to whose information Tom Swift had left home, had not said he was Ned Newton.

"He said," reported Miss Blair, "that he was speaking for you, Mr. Newton, as you were busy in the bank. Whoever it was, said you wanted Tom to meet you at the Kanker farm. I heard that much over the wire, and naturally supposed the message came from you."

"Well, that puts a little different face on it," said Mr. Damon. "Tom wasn't deceived by the voice, then, for he must have thought it was some one speaking for you, Ned."

"But the situation is serious, just the same," declared Ned. "Tom has gone to keep an appointment I never made, and the question is with whom will he keep it?"

"That's it!" cried the eccentric man. "Probably some of those scoundrels were waiting at the farm for him, and they've got him no one knows where by this time!"

"Oh, hardly as bad as that," suggested Ned. "Tom is able to look out for himself. He'd put up a big fight before he'd permit himself to be carried off."

"Well, what do you think did happen?" asked Mr. Damon.

"I think they wanted to get him out to the farm to see if they couldn't squeeze some more money out of him," was the answer. "Tom was pretty easy in that barn business, and I guess Kanker was sore because he haven't asked a larger sum. They knew Tom wouldn't come out on their own invitation, so they forged my name, so to speak."

"Can you get Tom back?" asked Mrs. Baggert anxiously.

"Of course!" declared Ned, though it must be admitted he spoke with more confidence than he really felt. "We'll begin the search right away."

"And if I can get my hands on any of those villains—" spluttered Mr. Damon, dancing around, as Mrs. Baggert said, "like a hen on a hot griddle," which seemed to describe him very well, "if I can get hold of any of those scoundrels, I'll—I'll—Bless my collar button, I don't know what I will do! Come on, Ned!"

"Yes, I guess we'd better get busy," agreed the young bank clerk. "Tom has gone somewhere, that's certain, and under a misapprehension. It may be that we are needlessly alarmed, or they may mean bad business. At any rate, it's up to us to find Tom."

In Ned's runabout, which was a speedier car than that of the eccentric man, the two set off for Kanker's farm. On the way they stopped at various places in town, where Tom was in the habit of doing business, to inquire if he had been seen.

But there was no trace of him. The next thing to do was to learn if he had really started for the Kanker farm.

"For if he didn't go there," suggested Ned, "it will look funny for us to go out there making inquiries about him. And it may be that after he got that message Tom decided not to go."

Accordingly they made enough inquiries to establish the fact that Tom had started for the farm of the rascally Kanker, who had been so insistent in the matter of his almost worthless barn.

A number of people who knew Tom well had seen him pass in the direction of Kanker's place, and some had spoken to him, for the young inventor was well known in the vicinity of Shopton and the neighboring towns.

"Well, out to Kanker's we'll go!" decided Ned. "And if anything has happened to Tom there—well, we'll make whoever is responsible wish it hadn't!"

"Bless my fountain pen, but that's what we will!" chimed in Mr. Damon.

And so the two began the search for the missing youth.

Chapter XXI A Prisoner

Amos Kanker came to the door of his farmhouse as Ned and Mr. Damon drove up in the runabout. There was an unpleasant grin on the not very prepossessing face of the farmer, and what Ned thought was a cunning look, as he slouched out and asked:

"Well, what do you want? Come to smash up any more of my barns at three thousand dollars a smash?"

"Hardly," answered Ned shortly. "Your prices are too high for such ramshackle barns as you have. Where's Tom Swift?" he asked sharply.

"Huh! Do you mean that young whipper-snapper with his big traction engine?" demanded Mr. Kanker.

"Look here!" blustered Mr. Damon, "Tom Swift is neither a whipper-snapper nor is his machine a traction engine. It's a war tank."

"That doesn't matter much to me," said the farmer, with a grating laugh. "It looks like a traction engine, though it smashes things up more'n any one I ever saw."

"That isn't the point," broke in Ned. "Where is my friend, Tom Swift? That's what we want to know."

"Huh! What makes you think I can tell you?" demanded Kanker.

"Didn't he come out here?" asked Mr. Damon.

"Not as I knows of," was the surly answer.

"Look here!" exclaimed Ned, and his tones were firm, with no bluster nor bluff in them, "we came out here to find Tom Swift, and we're going to find him! We have reason to believe he's here—at least, he started for here," he substituted, as he wished to make no statement he could not prove. "Now we don't claim we have any right to be on your property, and we don't intend to stay here any longer than we can help. But we do claim the right, in common decency, to ask if you have seen anything of Tom. There may have been an accident; there may have been foul play; and there may be international complications in this business. If there are, those involved won't get off as easily as they think. I'd advise you to keep a civil tongue in your head and answer our questions. If we have to get the police and detectives out here, as well as the governmental department of justice, you may have to answer their questions, and they won't be as decent to you as we are!"

"Hurray!" whispered Mr Damon to Ned. "That's the way to talk!"

And indeed the forceful remarks of the young bank clerk did appear to have a salutary effect on the surly farmer. His manner changed at once and his grin faded.

"I don't know nothing about Tom Swift or any of your friends," he said. "I've got my farm work to do, and I do it. It's hard enough to earn a living these war times without taking part in plots. I haven't seen Tom Swift since the trouble he made about my barn."

"Then he hasn't been here to-day?" asked Ned.

"No; and not for a good many days."

Ned looked at Mr. Damon, and the two exchanged uneasy glances. Tom had certainly started for the Kanker farm, and indeed had come to within a few miles of it. That much was certain, as testified to by a number of residents along the route from Shopton, who had seen the young inventor passing in his car.

Now it appeared he had not arrived. The changed air of the farmer seemed to indicate that he was speaking the truth. Mr. Damon and Ned were inclined to believe him. If they had any last, lingering doubts in the matter, they were dispelled when Mr. Kanker said:

"You can search the place if you like. I haven't any reason to feel friendly toward you, but I certainly don't want to get into trouble with the Government. Look around all you like."

"No, we'll take your word for it," said Ned, quickly concluding that now they had got the farmer where they wanted him, they could gain more by an appearance of friendliness than by threats or harsh words. "Then you haven't seen him, either?"

"Not a sign of him."

"One thing more," went on Tom's chum, "and then we'll look farther. Weren't you induced by a man named Simpson, or one named Blakeson, to make the demand of three thousand dollars' damage for your barn?"

"No, it wasn't anybody of either of those names," admitted Mr. Kanker, evidently a bit put out by the question.

"It was some one, though, wasn't it?" insisted Ned.

"Waal, a man did come to me the day the barn was smashed, and just afore it happened, and said an all-fired big traction engine was headed this way, and that a young feller who was half crazy was running it. This man—I don't know who he was, being a stranger to me—said if the engine ran into any of my property and did damages I should collect for it on the spot, or hold the machine.

"Sure enough, that's what happened, and I did it. That man had an auto, and he brought me and some of my men out to the smashed barn. That's all I know about it."

"I thought some one put you up to it," commented Ned. "This was some of the gang's work," he went on to Mr. Damon. "They hoped to get possession of Tom's tank long enough to find out some of the secrets. By having the Liberty Bonds, I fooled 'em."

"That's what you did!" said Mr. Damon. "But what can we do now?"

"I don't know," Ned was forced to admit. "But I should think we'd better go back to the last place where he was seen to pass in his auto, and try to get on his trail."

Mr. Damon agreed that this was a wise plan, and, after a casual look around the farmhouse and other buildings on Kanker's place and finding nothing to arouse their suspicions, the two left in Ned's speedy little machine.

"It is mighty queer!" remarked the young bank clerk, as they shot along the country road. "It isn't like Tom to get caught this way."

"Maybe he isn't caught," suggested the other. "Tom has been in many a tight place and gotten out, as you and I well know. Maybe it will be the same now, though it does look suspicious, that fake message coming from you."

"Not coming from me, you mean," corrected Ned. "Well, we'll do the best we can."

They proceeded back to where they had last had a trace of Tom in his machine, and there could only confirm what they had learned at first, namely, that the young inventor had departed in the direction of the Kanker farm, after having filled his radiator with water, and chatting with a farmer he knew.

"Then this is where the trail divides," said Ned, as they went back over the road, coming to a point where the highway branched off. "If he went this way, he went to Kanker's place, or he would be in the way of going. He isn't there, it seems, and didn't go there."

"If he took the other road, where would he go?" asked Mr. Damon.

"Any one of a dozen places. I guess we'll have to follow the trail and make all the inquiries we can."

But from the point where the two roads branched, all trace of Tom Swift was lost. No one had seen him in his machine, though he was known to more than one resident along the highway.

"Well, what are we going to do?" asked Mr. Damon, after they had traveled some distance and had obtained no news.

"Suppose we call up his home," suggested Ned, as they came to a country store where there was a telephone. "It may be he has returned. In that case, all our worry has gone for nothing."

"I don't believe it has," said Mr. Damon. "But if we call up and ask if Tom is back it will show we haven't found him, and his father will be more worried than ever."

"We can ask the telephone girl, and tell her to keep quiet about it," decided Ned; and this they did.

But the answer that came back over the wire was discouraging. For Tom had not returned, and there was no word from him. There was an urgent message for him, too, from government officials regarding the tank, the girl reported.

"Well, we've just got to find him—that's all!" declared Ned. "I guess we'll have to make a regular search of it. I did hope we'd find him out at the Kanker farm. But since he isn't there, nor anywhere about, as far as we can tell, we've got to try some other plan."

"You mean notify the authorities?"—asked Mr. Damon.

"Hardly that—yet. But I'll get some of Tom's friends who have machines, and we'll start them out on the trail. In that way we can cover a lot of ground."

Late that afternoon, and far into the night, a number of the friends of Tom and Ned went about the country in automobiles, seeking news of the young inventor. Mr. Swift became very anxious over the non-return of his son, and felt the authorities should be notified; but as all agreed that the local police could not handle the matter and that it would have to be put into the hands of the United States Secret Service, he consented to wait for a while before doing this.

All the next day the search was kept up, and Ned and Mr. Damon were getting discouraged, not to say alarmed, when, most unexpectedly, they received a clew.

They had been traveling around the country on little-frequented roads in the hope that perhaps Tom might have taken one and disabled his machine so that he was unable to proceed.

"Though in that case he could, and would, have sent word," said Ned.

"Unless he's hurt," suggested Mr. Damon.

"Well, maybe that is what's happened," Ned was saying, when they noticed coming toward them a very much dilapidated automobile, driven by a farmer, and on the seat beside him was a small, barefoot boy.

"Which is the nearest road to Shopton?" asked the man, bringing his wheezing machine to a stop.

"Who are you looking for in Shopton?" asked Ned, while a strange feeling came over him that, somehow or other, Tom was concerned in the question.

"I'm looking for friends of a Tom Swift," was the answer.

"Tom Swift? Where is he? What's happened to him?" cried Ned.

"Bless my dyspepsia tablets!" exclaimed Mr. Damon. "Do you know where he is?"

"Not exactly," answered the farmer; "but here's a note from some one that signs himself 'Tom Swift,' and it says he's a prisoner!"

Chapter XXII
Rescued

For a moment Ned and Mr. Damon gazed at the farmer in his rattletrap of an auto, and then they looked at the fluttering piece of paper in his hand. Thence their gaze traveled to the ragged and barefoot lad sitting beside the farmer.

"I found it!" announced the boy.

"Found what?" asked Ned.

"That there note!"

Without asking any more questions, reserving them until they knew more about the matter, Mr. Damon and Ned each reached out a hand for the paper the farmer held. The latter handed it to Ned, being nearest him, and at a sight of the handwriting the young bank clerk exclaimed:

"It's from Tom, all right!"

"What happened to him?" cried Mr. Damon. "Where is he? Is he a prisoner?"

"So it seems," answered Ned. "Wait, I'll read it to you," and he read:

"'Whoever picks this up please send word at once to Mr. Swift or to Ned Newton in Shopton, or to Mr. Damon of Waterfield. I am a prisoner, locked in the old factory. Tom Swift'."

"Bless my quinine pills!" cried Mr Damon. "What in the world does it mean? What factory?"

"That's just what we've got to find out," decided Ned. "Where did you get this?" he asked the farmer's boy.

"Way off over there," and he pointed across miles of fields. "I was lookin' for a lost cow, and I went past an old factory. There wasn't nobody in the place, as far as I knowed, but all at once I heard some one yell, and then I seen something white, like a bird, sail out of a high window. I was scared for a minute, thinkin' it might be tramps after me."

"And what did you do, Sonny?" asked Mr. Damon, as the boy paused.

"Well, after a while I went to where the white thing lay, and I picked it up. I seen it was a piece of paper, with writin' on it, and it was wrapped around part of a brick."

"And did you go near the factory to find out who called or who threw the paper out?" Ned queried.

"I didn't," the boy answered. "I was scared. I went home, and didn't even start to find the lost cow."

"No more he did," chimed in the farmer. "He come runnin' in like a whitehead, and as soon as I saw the paper and heard what Bub had to say, I thought maybe I'd better do somethin'."

"Did you go to the factory?" asked Ned eagerly.

"No. I thought the best thing to do would be to find this Mr. Swift, or the other folks mentioned in this letter. I knowed, in a general way, where Shopton was, but I'd never been there, doing my tradin' in the other direction, and so I had to stop and ask the road. If you can tell me—"

"We're two of the persons spoken of in that note," said Mr. Damon, as he mentioned his name and introduced Ned. "We have been looking for our friend Tom Swift for two days now. We must find him at once, as there is no telling what he may be suffering."

"Where is this old factory you speak of," continued Mr. Damon, "and how can we get there? It's too bad one of you didn't go back, after finding the note, to tell Tom he was soon to be rescued."

"Waal, maybe it is," said the farmer, a bit put out by the criticism. "But I figgered it would be better to look up this young man's friends and let them do the rescuin', and not lose no time, 'specially as it's about as far from my place to the factory as it is to Shopton."

"Well, I suppose that's so," agreed Ned. "But what is this factory?"

"It's an old one where they started to make beet sugar, but it didn't pan out," the farmer said. "The place is in ruins, and I did hear, not long ago, that somebody run a threshin' machine through it, an' busted it up worse than before."

"Great horned toads!" cried Ned. "That must be the very factory Tom ran his tank through. And to think he should be a prisoner there!"

"Held by whom, do you suppose?" asked Mr. Damon.

"By that Blakeson gang, I imagine," Ned answered. "There's no time to lose. We must go to his rescue!"

"Of course!" agreed Mr. Damon. "We're much obliged to you for bringing this note," he went on to the farmer. "And here is something to repay you for your trouble," and he took out his wallet.

"Shucks! I didn't do this for pay!" objected the farmer. "It's a pity I wouldn't help anybody what's in trouble! If I'd a-knowed what it meant, me and Bub here would have gone to the factory ourselves, maybe, and done the work quicker. But I didn't know—what with war times and such-like—but that it would be better to deliver the note."

"It turns out as well, perhaps," agreed Ned. "We'll look after Tom now."

"And I'll come along and help," said the farmer. "If there's a gang of tramps in that factory, you may need some reinforcements. I've got a couple of new axe handles in my machine, and they'll come in mighty handy as clubs."

"That's so," said Mr. Damon. "But I fancy Tom is simply locked in the deserted factory office, with no one on guard. We can get him out once we get there, and we'll be glad to have you come with us. So if you won't take any reward, maybe your boy will, as he found the note," and Mr. Damon pressed some bills into the hands of the boy, who, it is needless to say, was glad to get them.

It was a run of several miles back to the deserted factory, and though they passed houses on the way, it was decided that no addition to their force was necessary, though they did stop at a blacksmith shop, where they borrowed a heavy sledge to batter down a door if such action should be needed.

The farmer's rattletrap of a car, in spite of its appearance, was not far behind Ned's runabout, and in a comparatively short time all were within sight of the ruined place—a ruin made more complete by the passage through it of Tom Swift's war tank.

"And to think of his being there all this while!" exclaimed Mr. Damon, as he and Ned leaped from their machine.

"If he only is there!" murmured the young bank clerk.

"What do you mean? Didn't the note he threw out say he was there?"

"Yes, but something may have happened in the meanwhile. Those plotters, if they'd do a thing like this, are capable of anything. They may have kidnapped Tom again."

"Anyway, we'll soon find out," murmured Ned, as they advanced toward the ruin, Mr. Damon and the farmer each armed with an axe helve, while Ned carried the blacksmith's sledge.

They went into the end of the factory that was less ruined than the central part, where the tank had crashed through, and made their way into what had been the office—the place where they had found the burned scraps of paper.

"Hark!" exclaimed Ned, as they climbed up the broken steps. "I heard a noise."

"It's him yellin'—like he did afore he threw out the note," said the boy. Then, as they listened, they heard a distant voice calling:

"Hello! Hello, there! If that is any friend of mine, let me out, or send word to Mr. Damon or Ned Newton! Hello!"

"Hello yourself, Tom Swift!" yelled Ned, too delighted to wait for any other confirmation that it was his friend who was shouting. "We've come to rescue you, Tom!"

There was a moment of silence, and then a voice asked:

"Who is there?"

"Ned Newton, Mr. Damon, and some other friends of yours!" answered the young bank clerk, for surely the farmer and his son could be called Tom's friends.

An indistinguishable answer came back, and then Ned cried:

"Where are you, Tom? Tell us, so we can get you out!"

They all listened, and faintly heard:

"I'm in some sort of an old vault, partly underground. It's below what used to be the office. There's a flight of steps, but be careful, as they're rotten."

Eagerly they looked around Mr. Damon saw a door in one corner of the office, and tried to open it. It was locked, but a few blows from the sledge smashed it, and then some steps were revealed.

Down these, using due caution, went Ned and the others, and at the bottom they came upon another door. This was of sheet iron and was fastened on the outside by a big padlock.

"Stand back!" cried Ned, as he swung the sledge, and with a few blows broke the lock to pieces.

Then they pulled open the door, and into the light staggered Tom Swift, a most woe-begone figure, and showing the effects of his imprisonment. But he was safe and unharmed, though much disheveled from his attempts to escape.

"Thank Heaven, you've come!" he murmured, as he clasped Ned's hand. "Is the tank all right?"

"All right!" cried Ned. "And now tell us about yourself. How in the world did you get here?"

"It's quite a yarn," answered Tom. "I've got to pull myself together before I answer," and he sank wearily down on a step, looking very haggard and worn.

Chapter XXIII
Gone

"Here, eat some of this," and Ned held something out to his chum. "It'll bring you up quicker than anything else, except a cup of hot tea, and we'll get that as soon as you can get away from here," went on the young bank clerk.

"What is it?" Tom asked, and his voice was very weary.

"It's a mixture of chocolate and nuts," replied Ned. "It's a new form of emergency ration issued to soldiers before they go over the top. Our Y.M.C.A. is sending a lot to the boys from around here who are in France. I was helping pack the boxes ready for shipment, and I kept out some to show you. Lucky I had it with me. Eat it, and you'll feel a lot better in a few minutes. You haven't had much to eat, have you?"

"Very little," answered Tom, as he nibbled half-heartedly at the confection Ned gave him, while Mr. Damon went out to the automobile and came back with a thermos bottle filled with cool water. He always provided himself with this on taking an automobile trip.

Tom managed to eat some of the chocolate, and then took a drink of the cool water. In a little while he declared that he felt better.

"Then come out of here!" exclaimed Ned. "You can tell us how it all happened and what they did to you. But I can see that last—they treated you like a dog, didn't they?"

"Pretty nearly," answered Tom; "but they didn't have things all their own way. I think I made one or two of them remember me," and he glanced at his swollen and bruised hands. Indeed, he bore the marks of having been in a fierce fight.

"Are you sure the tank's all right?" he asked Ned again. "That has been worrying me more than my own condition. I could think of only one reason why they got me here and held me prisoner, and that was to get me out of the way while they captured my tank. Then they haven't got her?" he asked eagerly.

"Not a look at her," Ned answered. "She was safe in the shop when we set out this morning."

"And now it's late afternoon," murmured Tom. "Well, I hope nothing has happened since," and there was vague alarm in his voice, an alarm at which Ned and Mr. Damon wondered.

"Couldn't you stop at some farmhouse and get fixed up a little?" asked Mr. Kimball, the farmer who had brought the note to Ned and Mr. Damon.

"I need to get fixed up somewhere," replied Tom, with a rueful look at himself—his hands, his torn clothes, and his general dilapidated appearance. "But I don't want to lose any time. I'm afraid something has happened at home, Ned."

"Nonsense! How could there, with Koko on guard, to say nothing of Eradicate!"

"Well, maybe you're right," agreed Tom; "but I'll feel better when I see my tank in her shed. Let's have some more of that concentrated porterhouse steak of yours, Ned. It is good, and it fills out my stomach, which was getting more intimate with my backbone than I liked to feel."

More of the really good confection and another drink of refreshing water made Tom feel better, and he was soon able to walk along without staggering from weakness.

"And now let's get out of here," advised Ned, "unless you've left something back in that vault you want, Tom," and he motioned to his chum's late prison.

"Nothing there but bad memories," was the reply, with a rueful smile. "I'm as ready to go as you are, Ned. It was good of you and Mr. Damon to come for me, and you"—and he looked questioningly at Mr. Kimball.

"If it hadn't been for Mr. Kimball and his boy, we wouldn't have found you—at least so soon," said Ned, and he told of the finding of the note and what had followed.

"That's the only way I could think of for getting help," said Tom. "They took every scrap of paper from me, but I found some in the lining of my hat—some I'd stuffed in after I had a hair cut and my hat was too large. For a pencil I used burnt matches. Oh, but I'm glad to be out!" and he breathed deep of the fresh air.

"How did you get in there?" asked Ned wonderingly.

"Those fellows—of course. The German plotters, I'm going to call them, for I believe that Blakeson and his gang—though I didn't see him—are really working in the interests of Germany to get the secret of my tank."

"Well, they haven't got her yet," said Ned, "and they're not likely to now. Go on, Tom, if you feel able tell us in a few words what happened. We've been trying to think, but can't."

"Well, it all happened because I didn't think enough," said Tom, who was rapidly recovering his strength and nerve. "When I got that message that seemed to come from you, Ned, I should have known better than to take a chance. But it seemed genuine, and as I had no reason to suspect a trap, I started off at once. I thought maybe Kanker had repented and was going to make amends for all the trouble he caused.

"Anyhow, I started off in my machine, and I hadn't got more than to the crossroads when I saw a fellow out tinkering with his auto. Of course I stopped to ask if I could help, for I can't bear to see any machinery out of order, and as I was stooping over the engine to see what was wrong I was pounced on from behind, bound and tied, and before I could do a thing I was bundled into the car—a big limousine, and taken away.

"The crossroads was as far as we could trace you," remarked Ned.

"Well, it wasn't as far as they took me, by any means," Tom said. "They brought me here, took me out of the machine—and I noticed that they'd brought mine along—and then they carted me into the vault.

"But they didn't have it all their own way," said Tom grimly. "I managed to get the ropes loose, and I had a regular knock down and drag out with them for a while. But they were too many for me, and locked me up in that place after taking away everything I had in my pockets."

"Were they highwaymen?" asked Mr. Kimtall.

"No, for they tossed back my money, watch and some trifles like that," Tom answered. "I didn't recognize any of the men, though one of them must have known me, for when they had me tied I heard one of them ask if I was the right party, and another said I was. I know they must belong to the same gang that Simpson, Blakeson, and Schwen are members of—the German spies."

"But what was their object?" asked Ned. "Did they try to force you to tell them the secrets of the tank?"

"No; and that's the funny part which makes me so suspicious," Tom answered. "If they'd tried to force something out of me, I would understand it better. But they just kept me a prisoner after taking away what papers I had."

"Were they of any value?" asked Mr. Damon.

"Not as regards the tank. That is, there was nothing of my plans of construction, control or anything like that, though there was some foreign correspondence that I am sorry fell into their hands. However, that can't be helped."

"And did they just keep you locked up?" asked Ned.

"That's about all they did. After the fight—and it was some fight!" declared Tom, as he recalled it with a shake of his head—"they left me here with the door shut. There must have been some one on guard, for I could faintly hear somebody moving about.

"I tried to get out, of course, but I couldn't. That vault must have been made to hold something very valuable, for it was almost as strong and solid as one in your bank, Ned. The only window was placed so high that I couldn't reach it, and it was barred at that.

"They opened the door a little, several times, to toss in once some old bags that I made into a bed, and next they gave me a little water and some sandwiches—German bologna sausage sandwiches, Ned! What do you think of that—adding insult to injury?"

"That was tough!" Ned admitted.

"Well, I had to put up with it, for I was half starved, and as sore as a boil from the fight. I didn't know what to do. I knew that you'd miss me sooner or later, and set out to find me, but I hardly thought you'd think of this place. They couldn't have picked out a much better prison to hold me, for, naturally, you wouldn't suppose enough of it was left standing, after my tank had walked through it, to make a hiding place.

"However, there was, and here I've been kept. At last I thought of the plan of sending out a message on the scrap of paper I could tear out of my hat. So I wrote it, and after several trials I managed to toss it out of the window. Then I just had to wait, and that was the hardest of all. The last twelve hours I've been without food, and I haven't heard any one around, so I guess they've skipped out and don't intend to come back."

"We didn't see any one," Ned reported. "Maybe they became frightened, Tom."

"I wish I could think that," was the answer. "What is more likely to be the case is that they're up to some new tricks. I must get back home quickly."

And after a stop had been made at a farmhouse belonging to a business acquaintance of Ned's, where Tom was able to wash and get a cup of hot tea, which added to his recuperative powers, the young inventor, with Ned and Mr. Damon, set out for Shopton.

Before Mr. Kimball started for his home, renewed thanks had been made to the farmer and his son for the part they had played in the rescue, and the young inventor, learning that the boy had a liking for things mechanical, promised to aid him in his intention to become a machinist.

"But first get a good education," Tom advised. "Keep on with your school work, and when the time comes I'll take you into my shop."

"And maybe he'll make a tank that will rival yours, Tom," said Ned.

"Maybe he will! I hope he does. If he comes along fast enough, he can help with something else I'm going to start soon."

"Whats that?" asked Mr. Damon.

"Oh, it's something on the same order, designed to help batter down the German lines," Tom answered. "I haven't quite made up my mind what to call it yet. But let's get home. I want to see that my tank is safe. The absence of the plotters from the factory makes me suspicious."

On the way back Tom told more of the details of the attack.

"But we'll forget about it all, now you're out," remarked Ned.

"And the sooner we get home, the better," added Tom. "Can't you get a little more speed out of this machine?" he asked.

"Well, it isn't the Hawk," replied Ned, "but we'll see what we can do," and he made the runabout fairly fly.

Mrs. Baggert was the first to greet Tom as they arrived at his home. She did not seem as surprised as either Tom, Ned or Mr. Damon expected her to be.

"Well, I'm glad you're all right," she said. "And it's a good thing you sent that note, for your father was so excited and worried I was getting apprehensive about him."

"What note?" asked Tom, while a queer look came into his face.

"Why, the one you sent saying you were detained on business and would probably not be home for a week, and to have Koku and the men bring the tank to you."

"Bring the tank! A note from me!" exclaimed Tom. "The plotters again! And they've got the tank!"

He ran to the big shop followed by the others. Throwing open the doors, they went inside. A glance sufficed to disclose the worst.

The place where the great tank had stood was empty.

"Gone!" gasped Tom.

Chapter XXIV
Camouflaged

Two utterances Tom Swift made when the fact of the disappearance of the tank became known to him were characteristic of the young inventor. The first was:

"How did they get it away?"

And the second was:

"Come on, let's get after 'em!"

Then, for a few moments, no one said anything. Tom, Ned, and Mr. Damon, with Mrs. Baggert in the background, stood looking at the great empty machine shop.

"Well, they got her," went on Tom, with a sigh. "I was afraid of this as soon as they left me alone at the factory."

"Is anything wrong?" faltered the housekeeper. "Didn't you send for the tank, Tom?"

"No, Mrs. Baggert, I didn't," Tom answered.

"But I don't understand," the housekeeper said. "A man came with a note from you, Tom, and in it you said to have him take the tank, with Koku and the men who know how to run it. We were so glad to hear from you, and know that you were all right, that we didn't think of anything else, your father and I. So he went out and saw that the tank got off all right. Koku was glad, for it's the first chance he'd had to ride in it."

"Who was the man who brought the note?" asked Tom, and he was striving to be calm. "To think of poor old dad playing right into the hands of the plotters!" he added, in an aside to Ned.

"Well, I don't know who the man was," said Mrs. Baggert. "He seemed all right, and of course having a note from you—"

"Who has that note now?" asked Tom quickly.

"Your father."

"Come on," and Tom led the way back to the house. "I'll have a look at that document, which of course I never wrote, and then we'll get after the plotters and the tank."

"She ought to be easy to trace," observed Mr. Damon. "Bless my fountain pen, but she ought to be easy to trace! She will leave a track like a giant boa constrictor crawling along."

"Yes, I guess we can trace her, all right," assented Tom Swift; "but the point is, will there be anything left of her? That's what I'm afraid of now."

Mr. Swift was still excited, but his worry had subsided as soon as he knew Tom was safe.

"The whole thing is a forgery, but fairly well done," Tom said, as he looked at the paper his father gave him—a brief note stating that Tom was well, but detained on business, and that the tank was to be brought to him, just where the bearer of the note would indicate. Koku, the giant, and several of the machinists, who knew how to operate the big machine, were to go with it, the note said.

"That made me sure everything was all right," said Mr. Swift. "I knew, of course, Tom, that plotters might try to get hold of your war secret, but I didn't see how they could if Koku and some of your own men were in possession."

"They couldn't—as long as they remained in possession," Tom said. "But that's the trouble. I'm afraid they haven't. What has probably happened is that under the direction of this man, who brought the forged note from me, Koku and the others took the tank where he directed them, thinking to meet me. Then, reaching the place where the rest of the plotters were concealed, they overpowered Koku and the others and took possession of the machine."

"They'd have trouble with Koku," suggested Ned.

"Yes, but even a giant can't fight too big a crowd, especially if he is taken by surprise, and that's probably what happened," remarked Tom. "Now the question is where is the tank, and how can we get her back? Every minute counts. If those German spies and their helpers remain in possession long, they'll find out enough of my secrets to enable them to duplicate the machine, and especially some of the most exclusive features. We've got to get after 'em!"

"They imitated your writing pretty well, Tom," Observed Ned, as he looked at the forged note.

"Yes; that's why they took all my papers away from me—to get specimens of my handwriting. I half suspected that, but I didn't quite figure out what their game was. Well, we know the worst now, and that's better than working in the dark. Now I'm going to have a bath and get into some decent clothes, and we'll see what we can do."

"Count on me, Tom!" exclaimed Ned. "I'll go the limit with you!"

"I knew you would, old man!"

"And me, too!" cried Mr. Damon. "Bless my open fireplace, but I'll send word to my wife that I'm not coming home to-night, and we can start the first thing in the morning, Tom."

"Yes; there isn't much use in going now, as it will soon be dark."

"How are you going to trace the tank, Tom?" asked Ned, when his chum had bathed and gotten into fresh clothes.

"I'm going to tour the country around here in an auto. The tank can make ten miles an hour, but that's nothing to what an auto can do. And we oughtn't to have much trouble in tracing her. No one whose house she passed would forget her in a hurry."

"That's so," agreed Ned. "But if they took her across country—"

"A different story," agreed Tom. "Come to think of it, maybe we'd better start to-night, Ned. We can make inquiries after dark as well as by daylight and get ready for an early morning hunt."

"Let's do it, then!" suggested his chum. "I'm ready. I'll send word that I'll not be home to-night."

"Good!" cried the young inventor. "We'll have an old-fashioned hunt after our enemies, Ned!"

"And don't leave me out!" begged Mr. Damon. Hurried preparations were made for the night trip. Tom ordered out one of his speediest, though not largest, automobiles, and told his helper to get the Hawk ready, to have her so she could start at a moment's notice if needed.

"You're not going in her, are you, Tom?" asked Ned.

"I may need her to-morrow for daylight hunting. If the tank's hidden somewhere, I can spot her from above more easily than from the ground. So if we get any trace of my machine, I can phone in and have the aeroplane brought to me."

"That's a good idea!"

Inquiry at the shop where the tank had been built and kept disclosed the fact that, in addition to Koku, three of Tom's men had gone in her to help manage the machine under the direction of the man who bore the forged note. That he was one of the plotters not hitherto observed by either Ned or Tom seemed certain.

"And they took Koku and some of the men merely to make it look natural and as if it were all right," Tom said. "Naturally that deceived my father, who thought, of course, that I was waiting for the machine. Well, it was a slick trick, Ned, but we may fool them yet."

"I hope so, Tom."

Night had fully fallen when Tom, Ned, and Mr. Damon started away in the touring car.

Out onto the road rolled the automobile. During the little daylight that had remained after his arrival at home and following the discovery of the loss of the tank Tom and Ned had traced it, by the marks of the big steel caterpillar belts, to the main road. It had gone along that some distance, just how far could not be said.

"But by using the searchlight of the auto we can trace her as long as they keep her on the road," said Tom. "After that we'll have to trust to luck, and to what inquiries we can make."

The touring car carried a powerful lamp, and by its gleams it was easy to trace for a time the progress of the ponderous tank. There was no need to make inquiries of persons living along the way, though once or twice Tom did get out to ask, confirming the fact that the big machine had rumbled past in a direction away from the Swift home.

"I had an idea they might have doubled on their tracks for a time, and backed her up just to fool us," Tom said. "They might do that, keeping her in the same tracks."

But this, evidently, had not been done, and the tank was making good speed away from the Swift house. They kept up the search until about midnight, and then a heavy rain began just before they reached a point where several roads branched.

"Luck's with them!" exclaimed Tom. "This will wash away the marks, and we'll have to go it blind. Might as well put up here for the night," he added, as they came to a village hotel.

It was evident that little more could be done in the rain and darkness, and there was danger of over-running the trail of the tank if they kept on. So they turned in at the hotel and got what little rest they could in their anxious state of minds.

Tom tried to be cheerful and to look for the best, but it was hard work. The tank was his pet invention, and, moreover, that her secrets should fall into the hands of the enemy and be used for Germany and against the United States eventually, made the young inventor feel that everything was going wrong.

The rain kept up all night, and this would make it correspondingly hard for them to pick up the trail in the morning.

"The only thing we can do is to make inquiries," decided Tom. "Fortunately, the tank can't easily be hidden."

They started off after an early breakfast. The roads were so muddy and wet that traveling was difficult and dangerous for the automobile, and they were disappointed in finding no one who had seen or heard the tank pass up to a point not far from the hotel where they had stayed overnight. From then on the big machine seemed to have disappeared.

"I know what they've done," Tom said, when noon came and they had found no trace of the ponderous war machine. "They've left the road and taken her cross country, and we can't find the spot where they did this because the rain has washed out the marks. Well, there's only one thing left to do."

"What's that?" asked Ned.

"Get the Hawk! In that we can look down and over a big extent of country. That's what I'll do—I'll phone for the airship. The rain is stopping, I think."

The rain did cease by the time one of Tom's men brought the speedy aircraft to the place named by the young inventor in his telephone message. There were still several hours of daylight left, and Tom counted on them to allow him to rise in the air and look down on the tanks possible hiding place.

"One thing's sure," he told Ned: "I know the limit of her speed, and she can't be farther off than at some place within a circle of about one hundred and twenty-five miles from my house. And it's in the direction we're in. So if I circle around up above, I may spot her."

"I hope so," murmured Ned.

It was arranged that Mr. Damon should take the automobile back, with Tom's mechanician in it, and Tom and Ned would scout around in the aircraft, which carried only two.

"You ought to have a machine gun with you, Tom, if you plan to attack those fellows to get back the tank," Ned said.

"Oh, I don't imagine I'll need it," he said. "Anyhow, a machine gun wouldn't be of much effect against the tank. And they can't fire on us, for there wasn't any ammunition for the guns in Tank A, unless they got some of their own, and I hardly believe they'd do that. I'll take a chance, anyhow."

And so the search from the air began. It was disappointing at first. Around and around circled Tom and Ned, their eyes peering eagerly down from the heights for a sight of the tank, possibly hidden in some little-known ravine or gully.

Back and forth, like a speck in the sky, Tom guided the Hawk, while Ned took observation after observation with the binoculars.

At last, when the low-sinking sun gave warning that night would soon be upon them, Ned's glasses picked up something on the ground far below that made him sit suddenly straighter in his seat.

"What is it?" asked Tom through the speaking apparatus, feeling the movement on the part of his chum.

"I see something down there, Tom," was the answer. "It doesn't look like the tank, and yet it doesn't look as a clump of trees and bushes ought to look. Have a peep yourself. It's just beyond that river, against the side of the hill—a lonesome place, too."

Tom took the glasses while Ned assumed control of the Hawk, there being a dual system for operating and steering her.

No sooner had the young inventor got the focus on what Ned had indicated than he gave a cry.

"What is it?" asked the young bank clerk.

"Camouflaged!" cried Tom, and without stopping to explain what he meant, he handed the binoculars back to Ned and began to guide the Hawk down toward the earth at high speed.

Chapter XXV
Foiled

"Is it really Tank A, Tom?" cried Ned, through the tube, as soon as he became aware of his companion's intention. "Are you sure?"

"That's the girl, and just where you spotted her with the glasses—in that clump of bushes. But they've daubed her with green and brown paint—camouflaged her, so to speak—until she looks like part of the landscape. What made you suspicious of that particular place?"

"The green was such a bright one in contrast to the rest of the foliage around it.'

"That's what struck me," Tom answered, as he continued to drive the Hawk earthward. "They thought they were doing a smart trick—imitating the tactics of the Allies with their tanks—but they must be color blind."

Ned took another observation through the glasses. He could see the tank more easily now. There she was, fairly well hidden in a clump of bushes and small trees on the banks of a river, about a hundred miles away from Shopton. It was in a wild and desolate country, and only with the airship could the trail have thus been followed.

Ned saw that the tank had been daubed with green, yellow, and brown paint, in fantastic blotches, to make the big machine blend with the foliage; and, to a certain extent, this had been accomplished.

But, as Ned had remarked, the green used was of too vivid a hue. No natural tree put forth leaves like that, and the glass had further revealed the error.

"Look, Tom!" suddenly cried Ned. "She's moving!"

"You're right!" answered the young inventor. "They've seen us and are trying to get away."

"But they can't beat your airship, Tom."

"I know that. But their game—Oh, Ned, they're going to wreck her!" cried Tom, and there was anguish in his voice.

As the two looked down from their seats In the Hawk they saw the tank, in its fantastic dress of splotchy paint, leave her lair amid the bushes and trees, and head toward the river. Like some ponderous prehistoric monster about to take a drink, she careened her way toward the stream, which, at this point, ran between high banks.

"What's the game?" cried Ned.

"They're going to send her to smash!" cried Tom. "She's pretty tough, Tom, but she'll never stand a tumble down into the river without breaking a lot of machinery inside her."

"But if they demolish the tank they'll kill themselves, won't they? And Koku and your men, too, who must be prisoners in her!"

"They won't risk their own worthless hides, you may be sure of that!" exclaimed Tom.

"There they go, but they must have left Koku and the others to their fate!"

"Oh, if they could only get loose and take control now, Tom, they'd save your tank for you!" shouted Ned.

"Yes; but they can't, I'm afraid. They may be killed, or so securely bound that they can't get loose!"

"Can't you get the Hawk there in time to stop her?"

"I'm afraid not. By that time she'll have attained top speed and it would be taking our lives in our hands to try to make a flying jump, get inside, and shut off the motors."

"Then the tank's got to smash!" said Ned gloomily.

Tom did not answer for a moment. He and his chum watched the fleeing figures running away from the war engine. What the plotters had done, as soon as they saw the aircraft and realized that Tom had discovered them, was to start the motors and leap from the tank, closing the doors after them. Whether or not they had left Koku and the others prisoners inside remained to be seen.

But the tank was plunging her way toward the steep bank of the river, doomed, it seemed, to great damage, if not to destruction.

"Oh, if we could only halt her!" murmured Ned.

Tom Swift was busy with some apparatus on the Hawk. Ned heard the hum of an electric motor which was connected with the engine, and there soon sounded the crackle of the wireless.

"What are you doing? Signaling for help from those inside the tank?" asked Ned, for the big machine was fitted to receive and send messages of this sort.

"I'm trying something more desperate than that," Tom answered.

Again the wireless crackled, Tom working it with one hand while, with the other, he guided the aircraft. Ned looked downward with wondering eyes.

The tank was still plunging her way toward the steep bank of the river. If she tumbled down this, there would be little left of the expensive and complicated machinery inside.

"The rascals did their work well," mused Ned. "They've probably gotten all the secrets they want and now they're going to spoil all Tom's hard work. It's a shame! If only—"

Ned ceased his musing. Something was taking place down below that he could not explain. The tank seemed to be slackening her progress. More and more slowly she approached the edge of the cliff.

"Tom! Tom!" yelled Ned. "You must have waked some of them up inside and they've thrown the motors out of gear! Hurrah! She's stopping!"

"I believe she is!" yelled Tom. "Oh, if it only works!"

The tank was still moving, though more slowly. Still the crackle of the wireless was heard.

And then, just as Tom shut off his own motor and let the Hawk glide on her downward way in a volplane to earth, the great, ponderous tank came to a stop, on the very edge of the precipice at the foot of which rolled the river.

"Whew!" whistled Ned, as the aircraft rolled along the ground near the war machine. "That was touch and go, Tom! They stopped her just in time."

"You mean the wireless stopped her," said Tom quietly. "I'm very much afraid that if Koku and the others are alive they're still prisoners in the craft."

"The wireless!" gasped Ned, as he and his chum got out of the Hawk. "Do you mean that you stopped her by wireless, Tom?"

"That's what I did. It was a desperate chance, but I took it. I had just installed in the tank a system of wireless control, so she could be guided as some torpedos and submarines are, by wireless impulses from the shore.

"Only I'd never given the tank system a tryout. It was all installed, and had worked perfectly on the small model I constructed. And when I saw her running away, out of control as she was, I realized the wireless was the only thing that would stop her, if that would. It might operate just opposite to what I wanted, though, and increase her speed."

"But I took the chance. I set the airship wireless current to working, and tuned it in to coincide with the control of the tank. Then, by means of the wireless impulse I shut off the motors, which can be stopped or started by hand or by electricity. I shut 'em off."

"And only just in time!" cried Ned. "Whew, Tom Swift, but that was a close call!"

"I realize that myself!" said the young inventor. "This is a new idea and has to be worked out further for our newer tanks."

"Gee!" ejaculated Ned. "Out of date before got into use! Now let's see about our friends!"

It was the work of but a moment to enter the tank, and, after making sure that the machinery was all right, Tom and Ned made their way to the interior. In one of the smallest rooms they found Koku and the others bound with ropes, and in a bad way. Koku was so tied with cords and hemp as to resemble a bale of Manilla cable.

"Cut 'em loose, Ned!" cried Tom, and the bonds were soon severed. Then came explanations.

As has been told, one of the plotters, whose identity was not learned until later, came with the forged note. The giant and Tom's men set out in the tank, and the machine was stopped at a certain place where the plotter, who gave the name of Crossleigh, told them Tom was to meet his men.

Out of ambush leaped Simpson and others, who overpowered the mechanics, even subduing Koku after a fierce fight, and then they took possession of the tank, making the others prisoners.

What happened after that could only be conjectured by Tom's men, for they were shut up in an inner room. It seemed certain, though, that the tank was taken to some secret place and there painted to resemble the verdure. Then she went on again, coming to rest where Tom and Ned saw her.

Meanwhile the plotters were gradually getting at the secrets of construction, and they were in the midst of this work when one of them saw the aeroplane.

Rightly guessing what it portended, they left hurriedly, still leaving the hapless men bound, and started the tank on what they thought would be her last trip.

"But you saved her, Tom!" cried Ned. "You saved her with the wireless."

And word was sent back to Shopton by the same means to tell Mr. Swift, Mr. Damon, and the others that Tom and his tank were safe. And then, a little later, when the bound men had recovered the use of their cramped limbs, the tank was backed away from the ledge and started on her homeward way, Tom and Ned preceding her in the Hawk.

Without further incident, save a slight break which was soon repaired, Tank A soon reached her harbor again, and a double guard was posted about the shop.

"And they won't get much more chance to steal her secrets," said Tom that night, when the stories had been told.

"Why?" asked Ned.

"We start to dismantle her at once," Tom answered, "and she goes to England to be reproduced for France."

"If only those plotters haven't stolen the secrets," mused Ned.

But if they had they got little good of them. For shortly afterward government secret service agents rounded up the chief members of the gang, including Simpson and Blakeson. They, with Schwen, were sent to an internment camp for the period of the war, and enough information was obtained from them to disclose all the workings of the plot.

"It was just like lots of other stunts the German spies tried to put over on the good old U.S.A.," said Tom to Ned, the day after the dismantled tank was shipped to Great Britain. "In some way the spies found out what I was making, and then they got hold of Blakeson and Grinder. Those fellows, who so nearly queered me in the big tunnel game promised to make a tank that would beat those the British at first put out, and they took some German money in advance for doing it.

"When they found they couldn't make good, the German spies agreed to help them get possession of my secrets. They worked hard enough at it, too, but, thanks to you, Ned, and to Eradicate, who gave us the tip on Schwen, we beat 'em out."

"And so it's all over, Tom?"

"Yes, practically all over. I've given all my interests in the tank to Uncle Sam. It was the only way I could do my bit, at this time. But I've something else up my sleeve."

And those of you who care to learn what the young inventor next did may do so by reading the next volume of this series.

It was about a week after Tank A, as she was still officially called, had been shipped in sections that Ned Newton called at Tom's home. He found his chum, with a flower in his buttonhole, about to leave in his small runabout.

"Oh, excuse me!" exclaimed Ned. "This is Wednesday night. I might have known. Give Mary my regards."

"I will," promised Tom, with a smile.